DRESSED TO PLAY

DRESSED TO PLAY

Jennifer Manuel

James Lorimer & Company Ltd., Publishers
Toronto

Published in Canada in 2019. Published in the United States in 2020.

James Lorimer & Company Ltd., Publishers acknowledges funding support from the Ontario Arts Council (OAC), an agency of the Government of Ontario. We acknowledge the support of the Canada Council for the Arts, which last year invested $153 million to bring the arts to Canadians throughout the country. This project has been made possible in part by the Government of Canada and with the support of Ontario Creates.

Cover design: Tyler Cleroux
Cover image: Shutterstock

Library and Archives Canada Cataloguing in Publication

Title: Dressed to play / Jennifer Manuel

Names: Manuel, Jennifer, author.

Description: Series statement: Sports stories

Identifiers: Canadiana (print) 20190131012 | Canadiana (ebook) 20190131020 | ISBN 9781459414679 (softcover) | ISBN 9781459414686 (epub)

Classification: LCC PS8625.A69 D74 2019 | DDC jC813/.6—dc23

Published by:
James Lorimer &
Company Ltd., Publishers
117 Peter Street, Suite 304
Toronto, ON, Canada
M5V 0M3
www.lorimer.ca

Distributed in Canada by:
Formac Lorimer Books
5502 Atlantic Street
Halifax, NS, Canada
B3H 1G4

Distributed in the US by:
Lerner Publisher Services
1251 Washington Ave. N.
Minneapolis, MN, USA
55401
www.lernerbooks.com

Printed and bound in Canada.
Manufactured by Marquis in Montmagny, Quebec in July 2019..
Job #174004

For Dad,
Thank you for all those hours in the yard, the driveway, the courts.

Contents

1 Is She REALLY?

Jordan Connor ran across the top of the three-point line. She caught the bounce pass from the other guard on her team, Amin Haddad. She pivoted away from her check, Wyatt Nowack, and held the basketball tight against her hip. Sometimes at the end of practice, like today, the team coaches let the players scrimmage together, mixing up the girls and boys. As captain of the grade nine girls' team, Jordan liked practising with the boys' team. She felt it really helped her team's level of play.

With her back to the hoop, Jordan listened to the squeak of her teammates' shoes on the gym floor as they tried to cut open for a pass.

But nobody called for the ball. Jordan thought about what to do. It wasn't every day that she got to test her skills against the boys. And Wyatt Nowack was the best basketball player in grade nine for the White Rock Orcas, boys or girls.

Can I pull up a long shot from here? she wondered.

"Last minute!" Coach Banford called out.

Wyatt shuffled closer to Jordan. He crouched low, ready to spring if she tried to shoot.

Jordan tightened her grip on the ball. She swung it closer to Wyatt and he took the bait. He stepped forward and tried to poke at the ball with lightning-quick hands.

It gave Jordan the perfect chance to test her new move. It had to be bold, or it would never fool a player like Wyatt.

Looking over her left shoulder, Jordan made eye contact with her best friend, Samira Sandhu, who was trying to shake off her check.

"Samira!" Jordan yelled. She faked an overhead pass.

Wyatt waved his hand to block the ball, but he was watching for the fake. With a stutter step to the right, Jordan dribbled the ball low across her body. As soon as Wyatt lunged for it, Jordan pulled the ball backward through the air and around in a giant circle. She spun her body past Wyatt, brushing her shoulder against his. She raced to the hoop.

But Wyatt was too quick to give up. Like Jordan, he was captain of his Orcas team. Like Jordan, he worked harder than anybody on the court.

As Wyatt scrambled to get back into defensive position, Jordan whipped a behind-the-back pass right into Samira's hands. Before Wyatt could recover, Jordan cut past him a second time. Samira fired a bounce pass back to Jordan. It was a perfect give-and-go play. It was just like they'd practised a thousand times in Jordan's driveway.

Jordan felt a surge of excitement as she spied the empty lane to the hoop. Sure, she could make the easy lay-up shot. But she wanted to do something with more pizzazz.

Under the hoop she dribbled for a reverse lay-up. Hooking her arm backward, she put a spin on the ball as she shot. It hit the backboard with a light thud. Then it twisted from the sidespin and swished through the net.

Her team cheered.

Jordan tugged at her jersey a few times to fan her sweaty body. It was a replica jersey of her favourite WNBA team. The Phoenix Mercury jersey made her feel like a real basketball player. And its bright orange colour highlighted her dark skin in a way Jordan loved.

"Nice shot!" said Amin. He ran up and gave Jordan a high five.

Coach Banford clapped his hands. "Great practice, Orcas!"

"Yes, good job," said Coach Li, the coach of the boys' team. "See you all on Thursday at the game against Marriott. Remember, it's the big one."

As the other players wandered off the court, Samira said, "Our new play worked!"

"Perfectly!" Jordan picked up the ball and spun it on her finger. "Just wait until I show you our next one. Saw it during the Phoenix game last night."

"I'm always up for new plays," Samira said. She grabbed the ball from Jordan and tossed it into the ball bin. "We're going to need some against Marriott."

"Got that right," chimed in their teammate, Hazel Joe. "I'm working on my post play every day at lunch this week."

"Good, we'll need those inside shots from you," Jordan said. Jordan admired how seriously Hazel took the game. Hazel lived on the Semiahmoo Reserve and played on the outdoor court there every day. She was the best rebounder the Orcas had.

The girls' grade nine team was only a month into the season. So far, they'd won three games and lost one. Not bad, but this would be the first time in the season playing their cross-town rivals, the Marriott Mavericks. The game ahead worried Jordan. She'd heard the Mavericks were fast, with the best outside shooters in the league.

Jordan and Samira made their way down the hall to their lockers. Amin jogged past with a basketball in his hands. "That was a pretty sweet move, Jordan."

"Thanks." Jordan opened her locker.

On the inside of Jordan's locker door were magazine cut-outs of basketball player Diana Taurasi. Diana Taurasi dribbling down the court. Diana Taurasi making a jump shot. Diana Taurasi passing behind her back. Diana Taurasi was a guard for Phoenix. There were newer WNBA players who Jordan loved to watch, but

Diana Taurasi had been her favourite player since she was little.

Dropping her duffel bag to the floor, Samira opened the locker next to Jordan's. Samira loved playing basketball, too. But like the other girls in grade nine, her locker door was plastered with pictures of her favourite singers and TV stars. Samira also had pictures of two of her favourite Bollywood stars dressed in bright Indian clothing. Cute boys, mostly. No WNBA players.

Samira checked her face in the small mirror on her locker door. She whispered, "Wyatt's coming," as if it was something magical.

Three boys, including Wyatt, were headed up the hall toward them. Two of them laughed and pointed at Jordan.

"Shut up!" Wyatt yelled at his friends.

"Shut up about what?" asked Leo, a tall boy who played centre forward.

"About you getting beaten to the hoop by a girl?" added Jeff, a shooting guard. He laughed. "A girl!"

"Is she?" Wyatt asked.

"What do you mean?" Leo asked.

"Is she *really* a girl?" Wyatt asked. He said it in an extra loud voice, as if he wanted to make sure Jordan heard him. "Or is she just a jock?"

Jeff and Leo snickered.

Wyatt smiled. "Jordan the Jock."

2 A NEW PLAY

After school the next day, Jordan and Samira practised a new play in Jordan's driveway. Samira ran the play for the eighth time, dribbling deep to the lower post with Jordan close behind. Jordan circled tightly around Samira, using her as a pick against an imagined defence. As Samira pivoted away from the net, Jordan called for the ball outside the three-point line.

Samira passed it back out. Passing was Samira's strength. She launched a hard chest pass right into Jordan's hands. With a quick release, Jordan shot the three-pointer from between the shrubs that bordered the neighbour's yard.

The ball bounced off the hoop and missed.

Jordan groaned. "My outside shot needs more work."

"Still, it's a good play." Samira grabbed the ball and took a jump shot. She missed, too. "My shot is no good, inside or outside."

"You just need to bend your knees more," Jordan

offered. She showed Samira. "Extend your arm fully. Flick your wrist for a nice backspin."

"Maybe Wyatt can help me at lunch." Samira smiled.

"Wyatt?" Jordan rolled her eyes.

Samira shrugged. "He's the best player in the school."

Jordan frowned as she remembered what Wyatt had said near their lockers. *He was just being a poor sport*, she thought.

Jordan dribbled the ball between her legs three times. Then she pulled up a jump shot and drained it. "Let's run the play again," she said.

"Wyatt looks like he's been working out lately, don't you think?" Samira asked, as she caught Jordan's pass. "His arms are getting more muscly."

"I guess so. I don't know. I haven't really noticed."

Samira rested the ball on her hip. "He looked at me a few times during the scrimmage yesterday. Did you see?"

"No," said Jordan. Why were they talking about Wyatt? "I thought we were going to run the play again. At least pass the ball if you're not going to do anything with it."

"Well, he did look at me." Samira passed the ball. "I need to do something with my hair next time. It gets all fuzzy halfway through practice."

Jordan dribbled the ball to the top of the driveway. She said like an announcer, "Three seconds left in the game. Jordan Connor gets the ball. She shoots —"

They both watched the ball sail in a giant arc. It hit the rim, bounced straight up and dropped into the hoop.

"The crowd goes wild!" cheered a voice from behind.

Jordan turned to see Amin standing on the sidewalk. Amin was a point guard. He wasn't a star like Wyatt, but Amin moved the ball around the court quickly. Jordan knew Amin was a true team player, always looking to help his teammates score.

Wyatt is just a one-man show, Jordan thought.

"Can I play?" Amin asked. He tossed his duffel bag onto the grass.

"Sure," Jordan said, bouncing the ball to him.

The week before, Amin had showed Jordan where to find the safety goggles in Science class. Other than that, they'd only ever said a few words to each other as their teams practised.

"A game of one-on-one?" Amin asked.

Jordan looked at Samira sitting on an old tree stump at the edge of the lawn. "Never mind me," Samira said. "I need a break. Go ahead, you two play."

Amin brought the ball down the driveway. Jordan could feel his eyes on her, but she was focused on the ball. Amin pulled up a jump shot and sunk it.

Jordan took the ball to the top of the driveway and drove hard to the net. She dribbled behind her back just before leaping into a lay-up. Amin brushed up against her closely. She almost lost her balance but managed to score.

"Sorry about that," Amin said. "Definitely a foul."

The foul line was spray painted orange on the driveway. When Jordan's mom first saw it the year before, her face had turned red with anger. She hadn't managed to say anything except to ask, "What were you thinking?" Lucky for Jordan, it was her dad who'd put it there.

Jordan drained the free throw and turned around to get set up on defence.

The next time down the court, Amin missed a jump shot. The ball clanged off the rim and rolled onto the grass past Samira.

"Should I leave you two alone?" Samira whispered as Jordan came to retrieve the ball.

Jordan shot her a look. "No! Why?"

"He likes you," Samira said, wiggling her eyebrows.

Jordan blushed hotly. "You don't know that."

Just then Jordan's mother pulled into the driveway.

"Hello, Jordan. Hello, Samira." She slammed the door shut and popped open the trunk. She looked at Amin. "And who might this be?"

"This is Amin," Jordan said.

Her mom nodded. "Hello, Amin. I'm Dr. Connor."

"My mom's a dentist," Jordan said proudly. She smiled as big as possible, showing gleaming white teeth.

"Not a single cavity in these chompers."

Amin laughed. "Bet you floss every night."

"Better believe it," Jordan chuckled. "Ever since I had two baby teeth to floss between."

Jordan's mom started to rummage through the trunk of her car, and Jordan passed the ball to Amin. He tried to dribble it behind his back. But it hit his heel and rolled into the flower bed.

Jordan grabbed the ball before her mom could see it squish one of her small shrubs. Then she dribbled the ball and whipped it around behind her back.

"You have to pull it all the way around your hip, Amin," she said. "Or else you lose momentum. I kept practising until I got my arm curling right around my body." Jordan offered the ball to Amin. "Try it again."

Instead, Amin walked over to his duffel bag. He pulled out his phone and checked the time. "Actually, I'm late for dinner. I better get going."

He sounded nervous. It made Jordan feel nervous, too. So she tried to act like she wasn't. "Don't want to miss dinner!"

But her words came out too loud.

"Smooth," Samira teased her.

Jordan shrugged it off. Still, she couldn't stop smiling.

3 FAKE IT

Inside the house, Jordan sat at the kitchen table. Her mom stirred alfredo sauce with a wooden spoon. On the back burner, a large pot steamed as water heated to a boil. Whenever Jordan's mom cooked, she tied her hair up into a giant bun the size of a cantaloupe. Instead of her mom's straight hair and light skin, Jordan had her father's tight black curls and dark skin.

Without turning around, her mom said, "The ball doesn't belong on the table."

"Sorry." Jordan put the basketball on the floor. She wiped her hands together, dry and dirty from playing outside, then pulled off her sweatshirt to cool down.

"Maybe you should wash that shirt every once in a while." Her mom cast a sideways glance at the Mercury jersey she wore to every practice.

"I wash it," Jordan said.

Her mom raised her eyebrows. "Not sure how, when you wear it every time you play basketball. And you are playing basketball every minute of the day, it seems."

Jordan shrugged. "I like practising in it."

"Surely you have other clothes you can practise in."

"I don't feel the same in other clothes," Jordan said.

Her mother squinted at Jordan for a moment. As she often did, she looked like she couldn't make sense of Jordan. "So, who is this new *friend* of yours?"

Jordan winced. She could tell by her mom's tone. Her mom wondered if Amin was her boyfriend, not just her friend.

"He's on the boys' basketball team. And he's in my science class."

"It's pretty obvious he likes you."

"Mom," Jordan groaned.

"Grab the garlic bread out of that bag for me, will you?" Her mom tapped the spoon on the edge of the saucepan and nodded at the counter.

Her mom held the oven door open for Jordan to slide the bread in. Then she let it close with a bang. "Do you like him?"

Do I? Just wondering that made Jordan smile. She tried to twist her mouth down straight. The last thing she needed was for her mom to know she liked a boy. Her mom liked to give a lot of advice. Mostly when Jordan didn't want it.

As if on cue, her mom launched into advice mode. "You know, boys don't like girls to be better at sports than they are themselves."

"What?" Jordan sat back at the table.

"It's a hard thing for boys to handle."

"That's dumb," Jordan protested. "And not all boys are like that."

Her mom sighed. "Some boys might pretend it doesn't bother them. But it does. Trust me. Remember when you beat Carson at tennis when we were on holidays last year?"

How could Jordan forget? Her brother Carson got so mad when she won that he wouldn't talk to her for two days.

"And remember that time you tried to show Carson how to throw a football?" Her mom shut off the back burner and carried the pot to the sink. "It upsets boys when you show them how to do things like that."

"But what if I *know* how to do things like that?" Jordan muttered.

"Sometimes it's not worth the trouble."

"But he *couldn't* do it," Jordan said. Carson was away at Simon Fraser University. "Carson couldn't throw a spiral to save his life."

Pouring the noodles into a strainer, her mom shrugged. "It's silly, I know. But if you like Amin, you might think twice before showing him how to dribble behind his back."

Jordan's mom didn't like sports and had never played sports. She never watched sports on TV, saying it was a "huge waste of time." And she'd only ever gone to one of Jordan's basketball games. What did she know about it?

Jordan's face grew hot. "He didn't mind," she said.

"Are you sure? He left suddenly."

Jordan frowned. *Was Amin mad that I showed him how to dribble?*

Her mom went on. "Sometimes it's easier to let them think —"

"You want me to fake it?" Jordan couldn't believe what she was hearing. "Don't you want me to try my hardest?"

Her mom stared at her oven mitt. "Of course, I do, Jordan."

"Then I don't get it," Jordan said.

Her mom sighed. "You will. Someday."

The front door flung open. Jordan's dad kicked off his boots the second he stepped inside the house. He looked worn out.

"How was practice, Jordan?" he asked, as he sank into the chair across from her.

"Good," Jordan said. "We scrimmaged with the boys' team. I scored the winning basket." Jordan glanced at her mom. She decided not to mention that it was a boy she'd beaten to the hoop.

"You used the new spin move?" her dad asked.

"You know it," said Jordan.

"Way to go," her dad said. Then he turned to Jordan's mom. "Smells great in here, Lois. Anything I can do to help?"

"Nope, just relax," she replied. "Should be ready in about ten minutes."

"Ten minutes," Jordan repeated, picking up the basketball. "Enough time for a quick game of Twenty-One, Dad."

Her dad rubbed his eyes hard. "All right, one game."

Outside, Jordan's dad went first. He scored four baskets in a row before Jordan even got a chance. Then she banked it in and took the ball out to the foul line. As she bounced the ball a couple of times, her dad made funny noises, trying to ruin her focus.

It worked. The ball rebounded off the hoop and landed in her dad's hands.

He pretended to cough, pointing out that she'd let the pressure get to her.

Jordan smiled. "Maybe if you didn't make all that noise —"

"It's good for you." Her dad winked. "You have to learn to play no matter what anyone else is saying or doing."

Her dad sunk the ball as he spoke. Not once had Jordan ever beaten her dad, not at any sport they'd ever played. And they'd played just about every sport. Tennis. Basketball. Soccer. Football. They'd turned everything into a competition. Even when Jordan was small, she couldn't remember her dad ever letting her win.

He wouldn't want me to fake it, she thought.

4 More Than a WARMUP ACT

It was the day of the Orcas' away games against the Marriott Mavericks. The gym was packed with Marriott students. Many wore crazy outfits, large hats, giant sunglasses. Some had painted their faces green and yellow, the Mavericks' team colours. It was one of the few games when the bleachers were packed with fans for both the girls' and the boys' games.

Jordan's skin prickled with excitement during the warmup. Now and then she glanced at the other end of the court. The Mavericks moved gracefully in a three-man weave. They looked perfectly coordinated. Their passes were crisp and on target every time.

On top of it all, the Mavericks wore real basketball jerseys — sleeveless white jerseys with dark green trim and bright yellow numbers. They even had matching shorts in the long style worn by the WNBA players. Jordan looked down at her jersey, with its short, fraying sleeves and faded blue colour. Jordan didn't feel dressed to play, not one bit.

Jordan jumped up and down on the spot as Coach Banford shouted out the starting lineup. The noise from the bleachers was so loud that Jordan wondered how her teammates would hear her call the plays. She wished her dad was there to see it, but he had a late shift at the pulp mill.

"Listen up," Coach Banford shouted. "The Mavericks and Orcas have been fierce rivals for more than a decade. You're going to hear a lot of cheering for them. And even more hollering against us. Do your best to tune it out."

As they walked onto the court, Jordan could feel something in the air of the Marriott gym, and it wasn't just the noise. There was a tension, like a thread being pulled too tight.

"Wyatt is here already," Samira whispered to Jordan. "How do I look?"

Jordan raised an eyebrow. "You look ready for a big game."

She glanced up at the bleachers where Wyatt and the rest of the White Rock boys team sat in their brand-new uniforms. They would play right after the girls. It seemed unfair to Jordan that the boys got new uniforms while the girls had to wear old, musty jerseys. Not to mention that the girls always played before the boys. As if they were nothing more than a warmup act for the real show.

Hazel positioned herself to take the tipoff. On either side of Hazel stood Mayleen and Petra. Samira was the other guard. As the ref approached with the ball, the girls called out the numbers of the Mavericks players they were going to check.

The ref blew the whistle. She tossed the ball into the air. Hazel lost the tipoff. The Mavericks guard Number 7, who was Samira's check, dribbled down the court. She handled the ball confidently, pounding it hard onto the floor. Samira moved with her, not letting her pass by. But Number 7 pulled up a quick shot from the outside and sunk a basket.

The crowd erupted in cheers.

Jordan shouted into Samira's ear. "Good defensive work. Just remember they're really good outside shooters. Tighten up your check just a bit."

Samira nodded. She passed the ball inbounds to Jordan and ran up the court.

Jordan called out the play. "Low Four! Low Four!"

Samira and Mayleen cut from the high posts to the low posts. They set screens for Hazel and Petra, who sprinted to the outside of the court. Jordan passed to Hazel and drove toward the net, looking for the give-and-go pass. But the Mavericks defence stayed tight on her. With no one else open, Hazel threw a risky pass across the court to Mayleen. Samira's check intercepted the pass and the Mavericks raced up the court, passing the ball and scoring an easy lay-up.

The crowd chanted, "Mav-er-icks! Mav-er-icks!"

Even though the Orcas had a poor start, Jordan felt

electrified by the game. She'd never played in front of such a big crowd before. Usually there was only a handful of students and parents in the stands for the girls' games. For the first time, Jordan felt like they were more than a warmup act for the boys. Clapping her hands, she turned to her teammates. "We got this, Orcas!"

Jordan called for a Low Four play again. This time, after the screens were set and Mayleen broke open, Jordan set a second screen on Mayleen's check. Mayleen dribbled past the screen and nailed a jump shot from the edge of the paint.

Jordan ran to Mayleen and raised both hands. She gave Mayleen a high five with each. "Way to go, Mayleen! Keep it up, team! Let's shut them down on defence."

The Orcas boys' team and a few students from White Rock Junior cheered. But their voices were small compared to the crowd's.

By half-time the score was 30–24 for the Mavericks. At the sound of the buzzer, the crowd rose to their feet and made the thumbs-down sign at the Orcas bench. They chanted, "Mavericks rule! Orcas drool!"

"How rude," Hazel said at the bench.

"I warned you," said Coach Banford. "They're going to do anything they can to throw you off your game."

Jordan reminded herself of her dad's words.

You have to learn to play no matter what anyone else is saying or doing.

5 What They Call CHEERING

"The Mavericks are awesome outside shooters," Coach Banford told his team before the start of the second half. "I know it's a tiring game. But stay low in your defensive stance and play them a little tighter. What do you see out there, captain?" he asked Jordan.

Jordan squirted water out of her bottle into her mouth. "Watch Number 8. She's really good at those inside passes. And Number 11 is going for the back-door pass almost every time. Tara, do you think you could come across the paint and double-team Number 16 when she gets the ball at the high post?"

Tara nodded. "You bet I can."

Jordan put her fist into the centre of the huddle to start a team cheer. "This game is ours, Orcas. You're all playing great. Let's keep each other going. On the count of three. One, two, three —"

"ORCAS!" the whole team cheered in unison.

The second half started no better than the first. The Orcas fell six more points behind. The Mavericks seemed refreshed and full of energy. But Jordan knew the Orcas looked exhausted. Jordan's legs felt heavy as she dribbled up the court. But she pushed on, scoring two outside shots in a row.

Somebody from the bleachers shouted, "Get Number 11! Don't let her shoot!"

Number 11 was Jordan's number. She smiled as she jogged back up the court to get set on defence.

By the fourth quarter, the Orcas were still down 48–42. But it was the Mavericks coach who called a time out.

"Just keep doing what you're doing," Coach Banford told his own team.

Jordan had a different idea, one that no one would like. "I know we're all really tired. But I think we should leave it all out there. Full court press."

Coach Banford raised his eyebrows.

"Go big or go home." Jordan shrugged.

The buzzer signaled the end of the time out.

The Orca players looked at one another. Nobody said a word until Samira gave a firm nod. "Go big or go home," she agreed. "Full court press."

An excited murmur went around the huddle.

Jordan switched up their usual cheer. "GO BIG!" she shouted.

"OR GO HOME!" her teammates shouted back.

Samira scored the next basket, and the Orcas moved into swift action. They picked up their checks right away instead of jogging back to their half of the court. They put defensive pressure on the Mavericks for the length of the whole court. It was tiring, but it took the Mavericks by surprise. They forced a bad pass. Jordan stole the ball right under the Mavericks net. She banked it off the backboard.

After several more plays up and down the court, the Orcas were down by just four points with two minutes left.

The Mavericks lobbed the ball to their tall centre, who stood strong at low post. She pivoted away from Hazel and shot a fade-away jumper. The crowded cheered. But the ball bounced off the hoop. Hazel snatched the rebound.

"Outlet!" Jordan shouted for the ball.

Hazel made an overhead pass right into Jordan's chest. Jordan raced up the court along the sidelines. She could feel the adrenaline through her limbs. Out of the corner of her eye she saw the whole crowd rise to their feet.

"Twenty seconds!" Mayleen shouted.

Jordan had dribbled just past the three-point line. When she heard Mayleen warn her of the time left, she backed up to shoot from outside the line.

She bent her knees deep. Extended her arm fully. Flicked her wrist for backspin. It was a perfect shot. Just as the ball was about to leave her fingertips, Mavericks Number 7 smacked Jordan hard on her shooting arm.

The ref blew the whistle for a foul. Every player on the floor stopped. All eyes were on the hoop.

Swish.

Jordan pumped her fist.

The ref motioned to the scorekeeper that the shot counted for three points. Then she pointed at the free-throw line. Jordan would get one free-throw shot.

The crowd fell silent.

From the bleachers, somebody yelled.

"Way to go, Jordan the Jock!"

Jordan flinched. She heard the words, but her mind was fixed on the foul shot she was about to take. In front of the huge crowd. If she scored this shot, they would tie the Mavericks. She took a deep breath as she stepped up to the free-throw line.

The crowd swayed back and forth. They tried to taunt Jordan. At first, they chanted, "Pressure! Pressure!" Then they chanted, "Miss, miss, miss!"

Jordan could hear something else, too. And even though she tried to block it out, she kept hearing it.

It was Wyatt.

"Jordan the Jock! Jordan the Jock!"

Jordan's stomach turned. She wiped her sweaty palms on her shorts before taking the ball from the ref. She bounced the ball a few times.

Just relax, she told herself.

The crowd hushed.

Out of the quiet, Wyatt shouted, "Jordan the Jock!"

Somebody else in the crowd laughed.

Then Wyatt, plus a few other voices, shouted it again. "Jordan the Jock! Jordan the Jock!"

Jordan clenched her jaw. She wished they would stop. They sounded like they were cheering for her. But what they shouted made her feel worse. She bounced the ball once more. Players leaned forward off the blocks, ready to fight for a rebound position.

"Jordan the Jock!"

Jordan put up the shot.

She missed so badly the ball didn't even hit the hoop. It bounced out of bounds.

The crowded shouted at once, "AIRBALL!"

Jordan's stomach dropped.

The ref blew the whistle and gave the ball to the Mavericks for an inbound ball.

There was not enough time left.

The buzzer went.

***

After the game, Samira and Jordan walked to the bus stop. "Tough loss," Samira said. She didn't say a word about Jordan's foul shot. "Next time we play them, at least we'll have our school cheering for us."

Jordan thought of Wyatt and the other Orcas up in the bleachers. "If that's what they call cheering," she said under her breath, "then I don't want to play."

Samira caught the end of what Jordan said and laughed. "You wouldn't miss a basketball game if it was the end of the world. The Mavericks fans were just trying to throw you off."

"The Mavericks fans weren't the problem," Jordan said. "It was Wyatt."

Samira shook her head. "He was cheering for you. I thought it was nice."

Since when is it nice to make fun of someone? Jordan thought.

"A lot of the boys were cheering for you," Samira said. "There was Stephen and Harjinder and Leo and Jeff —"

"Look, our bus is coming," Jordan interrupted.

But Samira wasn't finished. "And there was Amin."

Did Amin join in with the others? Jordan didn't want to think about it.

"Wyatt was the one who made me miss that foul shot," Jordan snapped. "Whose side was he on, anyways?"

Then she hurried to the bus stop before Samira could argue.

6 TOO MANLY

After practice on Tuesday, Coach Banford gathered the girls together. He clutched what looked like a thick magazine in his hands. "I know some of you have felt upset that the boys team has new uniforms. And ours —"

"Look like they're from the 1970s," Samira called out.

Everybody laughed and nodded.

"Our white home jerseys aren't even white anymore," added Mayleen.

"More of a delightful rainy day sidewalk colour," Hazel agreed.

"You'll be happy to know I've finally convinced the school to budget for new uniforms this year," said Coach Banford. "I wish we could have had them for the start of the season. But better late than never."

Jordan could hardly wait. She thought about the uniforms worn by the WNBA teams. She loved the tank-top style of their jerseys. It showed the players' strong shoulders when they stretched for a rebound or shot the ball. The jerseys were loose, and players wore them tucked into the long, baggy shorts that hung almost down to their knees. Some of them wore compression tights under their shorts. Maybe Jordan would buy a pair of tights with her savings.

"Anyhow, I'm leaving the decision up to you girls," Coach Banford said.

"We get to pick?" Samira's face lit up.

"That's right."

"Whichever ones we choose?" Mayleen asked.

"Whichever you choose." Coach Banford nodded. He handed the catalogue, some paper and a pen to Jordan. "Your captain here will be in charge of organizing your decision."

In the change room, Jordan passed around the catalogue. Small groups of girls hovered over it, pointing at pictures and flipping through pages. They made small noises and said, "Gross, not those ones," and "Ooh, yeah, I like those."

Jordan already had her heart set on the uniforms like those worn by the WNBA — loose and cool. She sat on the bench and drank from her water bottle.

Finally, the girls came to a decision. Petra brought the open catalogue to Jordan and pointed to a page. "Tell Coach Banford we choose these ones."

Jordan frowned. In the photo, the girl wore a jersey that looked more like a T-shirt than a basketball jersey. It was close-fitting and had tiny sleeves that covered the top part of her shoulders. Her matching shorts were not the long, loose style Jordan dreamed of playing in. Not at all. They were much shorter, tighter. They didn't even cover half the girl's thighs.

"We can't wear those. They aren't even real basketball uniforms." Jordan looked at the cover of the catalogue. She saw it contained all types of athletic wear. Then she flipped to the basketball section and held it up for everybody to see. "These are the basketball uniforms. You're supposed to pick from this section."

Tara shook her head. "That's not what Coach Banford said. He said whichever we choose. Besides, those uniforms aren't much different."

"They're totally different!" Jordan said. "We can't play in these. How are we supposed to move?"

"It's athletic wear," reasoned Mayleen. "It's for moving. And we don't like those basketball ones. They'll make us look ugly."

"We should be dressed to play," Jordan said. *Not playing dress up*, she thought.

"We'll be dressed to play. And we'll look fabulous, too." Petra pulled the elastic out of her ponytail, messed up her hair and posed like a model.

Everyone laughed.

Hazel stood up. "I agree with Jordan. This is basketball, not a fashion show."

"What's wrong with wanting to look good?" Samira asked.

"We *will* look good in proper uniforms," Jordan said.

"Not to the boys we won't," Samira argued.

"I don't play basketball for the boys," Jordan said.

"Me neither," added Hazel.

"What if we pick the uniforms we want as our home uniforms and the uniforms you want for our away uniforms?" Mayleen suggested. "They have to be different colours, anyways. Then everyone is happy."

Tara sneered. "I won't be happy."

"Besides," Petra said, "almost everyone on the team wants the cuter uniforms. Majority rules."

"Then we should have a secret vote on it," Jordan said. She tore up the paper into scraps and handed one piece to each player. "Pass this pen around. Write down which uniform you want. Hand your vote to me."

Next to Jordan, Samira wrote down her vote and passed the pen to Mayleen. As Samira handed the folded slip of paper to Jordan, she whispered, "Amin would think you look really cute in the uniforms we picked."

A warm feeling washed over Jordan. She liked the thought of Amin finding her cute. Still, she wanted to feel like a real basketball player.

When all the slips were handed to Jordan, she started to count the votes as everyone watched. Quickly she saw there wasn't any point in counting. Everyone except Jordan and one other person had voted for the uniforms Jordan didn't want.

She couldn't hide the disappointment in her voice.

"The T-shirt uniforms won."

The team cheered with excitement.

Everyone changed out of their sweaty practice gear. Samira tried to reassure Jordan. "Those other uniforms are too manly," she said. "We're girls."

Jordan remembered Wyatt had questioned whether she really was a girl. Her stomach tightened. "Oh, yeah, definitely," she said quickly. "Those uniforms are pretty sweet." She leaned sideways and dropped all the votes into the big garbage bin.

"Was it a close vote?" Hazel unlaced her sneakers.

Jordan shook her head. "Only two wanted the real uniforms."

"You and me." Hazel shrugged. "Oh well."

A small crowd of girls gathered around the mirrors. Some brushed pink onto their cheeks. Others applied mascara to their eyes. Jordan stood at the back of the crowd on her tiptoes to see into the mirror to comb her hair.

Looking at herself, Jordan wondered. *Why did Wyatt ask if I am really a girl? I don't look any different from the other girls. I wear the same kinds of clothes. My hair looks the same. What is it about me?*

Next to her, Samira pulled the lid off a stick of eyeliner. "It's my mom's," she explained to Jordan. "She said I could start wearing makeup."

Without giving it any thought, Jordan blurted, "Yeah, me too."

Samira laughed. "You?"

Jordan didn't like the surprise in Samira's voice. "Why not?"

"You just don't seem like the makeup type."

"What do you mean?"

"You're not exactly —" Samira hesitated. "You know. Feminine."

Jordan turned away, her cheeks growing hot.

Samira tried to soften her words. "It's just that you're really into sports."

"So are you," Jordan argued. She threw her comb into her bag.

"Not like you," Samira said.

Jordan snatched her bag and left the change room in a hurry. Instead of waiting for Samira at their lockers, she started to walk home by herself. Usually, if she didn't take the bus, Jordan dribbled her basketball all the way to school and home again. Three miles of crossovers. Behind her back. Between her legs. Spin moves around every stop sign. She was going to be the best player in White Rock Junior High. Maybe even in the Fraser Valley. And someday, the WNBA.

But this time she kept her ball in her duffel bag. She didn't feel like dribbling home today. She was too upset by a question that she couldn't push out of her mind.

Am I failing at being a girl?

7 Double the TROUBLE

At school the next day, Jordan walked to her classes with her head down. It had taken her an hour to put on eyeliner and mascara she had borrowed from her mom. Jordan was coordinated on the court, but her hand wasn't steady with makeup. She had messed it up a few times before getting it right.

In Social Studies class, Mayleen was the first to notice. "Jordan, you're wearing makeup!" she squealed.

Jordan didn't answer. She just stared at the map of Europe in her textbook. Wearing makeup made her feel like she was on display.

In Math class second block, Hazel said, "You look different today."

Jordan smiled shyly. She hoped Hazel meant it in a good way, but she couldn't tell for sure.

In Art class, Samira told her, "You look really pretty."

"Thanks," Jordan said. But part of her worried that Samira said it only because she felt guilty about what she'd said in the change room.

After school, Jordan got her things ready for their home game against the Elgin Eagles.

"You pumped for the game?" Amin asked. He was leaning against the locker next to Jordan's.

Startled, Jordan dropped her binder. Amin picked it up and handed it to her with a big smile. Being the daughter of a dentist, Jordan couldn't help but notice his teeth. She liked how both his incisors were slightly crooked.

"Going to be the top scorer again?" he asked.

"Again?" Jordan grabbed her shoes and her uniform from her bag. Coach Banford said the new uniforms would be there for next week's game. She hoped they'd get lost in the mail.

"You were the top scorer in the game against the Mavericks," Amin said.

Normally Jordan checked out the score sheet after every game. But for that game, she had been too upset about her missed free throw.

"How do you know?" Jordan asked.

It was the first time she'd seen Amin that day. When she turned to face him, he didn't even blink at her makeup. She was glad he didn't. She wasn't used to it herself.

"I counted." Amin shrugged.

"You counted for the whole game?"

Amin's face turned pink.

Mom was wrong, Jordan thought. *Amin wasn't mad*

about the dribbling. And he probably wasn't chanting with the other boys if he was busy counting my baskets.

"If you have a big game today," Amin said, "you'll be the top scorer in the league. The only player close to you is that Number 10 from the Mavericks. And they don't play today. It's all on the league website."

"There's a league website? I didn't know that."

At the end of the hall, the double doors burst open. It was Leo and Jeff.

"You coming, Amin?" Leo asked as they walked toward Jordan's locker. "We're doing some pregame conditioning in the parking lot."

Before Amin could answer, Jeff nudged Leo in the ribs and motioned at Jordan's locker door. Leo scanned the photographs of Diana Taurasi. He snickered and asked, "Is that a woman or a man?"

As they walked off, Leo laughed and said, "What a jock."

Jordan pretended not to hear.

Jordan saw that Amin must have heard Leo. But he pretended he didn't. "Good luck today," was all he said.

"You too," Jordan muttered.

Staring into her locker, she waited until Amin's footsteps faded down the hall. Then she wiped the tears from her eyes. Mascara smudged the outsides of her thumbs. Wearing makeup hadn't made a difference at all. They were still going to call her a jock. They were still going to act like she wasn't really a girl.

Is that what Amin thinks of me? she wondered.

Jordan grabbed one of the photos by its corner and pulled. She tore at the photograph of Diana Taurasi. But then she stopped halfway. She just couldn't do it.

Grabbing her gear, she slammed her locker door shut and hustled to the change room. She wanted to have an extra-long warmup before the game. Especially now that she had a chance to become the top scorer in the whole league.

★★★

From the starting jump ball, Jordan was on fire. The Elgin Eagles were a slower team than the Mavericks, and Jordan made the most of it. Their defence was loose and they left Jordan alone on the outside perimeter. By the end of the first quarter, Jordan had hit four three-pointers.

This game was quiet compared to the noise of the Mavericks crowd. The bleachers were empty except for a few players from the boys' team, including Amin, Leo and Jeff. Jordan breathed a sigh of relief. No Wyatt this time.

"Stack one!" Jordan called. She went to inbound the ball from the sidelines.

The Orcas quickly moved into a tight lineup in front of Jordan. The ref handed Jordan the ball. Jordan waited a second before smacking it hard with the palm of her hand. It was the signal for the Orcas to cut in four different directions. The stack confused the Eagles players. Jordan easily passed the ball to Tara, who dribbled it down the rest of the court for a breakaway lay-up.

Between every basket, Jordan tried to wipe off her mascara with the sleeve of her jersey. Maybe it was because she wasn't used to wearing makeup, but she didn't feel like a serious athlete with that stuff all over her face.

By half-time, Jordan had scored six three-pointers. The Eagles coach yelled at his players to check Jordan more tightly. Jordan realized that, if she could keep it up, she would reach her all-time highest game score.

"Keep pushing, Orcas," Jordan told her team. "Let's try to get every rebound. They're not an aggressive team. So let's get more physical under the net."

But the Eagles had a surprise for Jordan in the second half.

As soon as Jordan dribbled the ball past the half-court line, two Eagles players checked her. Jordan panicked and tried to force a pass. The Eagles forward intercepted it and took it down the court for a two-on-one breakaway.

"They're double teaming Jordan!" yelled Coach Banford. "Make sure you help her out!"

Jordan swelled with pride. *Double teamed? I am a force to be stopped!*

The next time down the court, Jordan was ready. If she was being double teamed, then one of her teammates was being left wide open. She eyed Samira off to the left, all by herself. Jordan hurled a baseball pass over the heads of the two players defending her.

Samira dribbled a few steps closer to the net and shot. Something about the way Samira moved seemed different to Jordan. But Samira sunk the basket, and Jordan put it out of her mind.

At the final buzzer, Orcas had won 56–32. Jordan had scored her personal best, twenty-one points. She was now the top scorer in the whole league.

"Awesome game, Jordan," said Leo as he strolled onto the court for the boys' warmup.

"Double teamed! How cool is that?" Jeff said. "You're double the trouble."

"Seven three-pointers." Amin shook his head with a smile. "Amazing."

"You've got a wicked outside shot," agreed Leo.

Jordan scrunched her eyebrows, confused. Two hours ago, Leo and Jeff were teasing her for being a jock and laughing at the photos on her locker door. How could they now be nice about the same thing they teased her for?

"Hey, Jordan," Hazel said as she wiped the sweat off her forehead. "Your dad said you guys could give me a ride home."

"Oh, sure," Jordan said. The Semiahmoo Reserve

was on the outskirts of town, in the opposite direction from Jordan's house. But Jordan didn't mind. It would give Hazel and Jordan a chance to review the game together.

"You aren't staying to watch our game?" Leo asked, looking at Hazel.

"Can't," Hazel said. "Have to babysit my little sister. Plus, the Lakers are playing the Celtics in a half hour."

Leo smiled at Hazel. "It's cool when girls like watching sports."

Jordan glared at Leo and bit the inside of her cheek. It was all she could do to keep from screaming.

8 Top of THE LEAGUE

On Saturday afternoon, it poured rain. It was a perfect day to stay indoors and watch the Phoenix Mercury game on TV.

Jordan got her favourite spot in the den ready. She had a fuzzy blanket, a bowl of popcorn and her phone within reach. On her phone, she'd pulled up their junior high school league website. Her name was at the top of a list. *Grade 9 Girls Top Scorers*. Smiling, she kept staring at her name.

She could hear the murmur of an old black-and-white movie her parents were watching in the other room. She had ten minutes before tipoff, so Jordan went into the other room.

"Check it out." Jordan held the screen in front of her dad's face.

"Would you look at that!" her dad said.

Jordan showed her mom.

"Way to go, Jordan," she said. "Guess all those hours of driving us crazy bouncing the ball in the driveway have paid off."

Jordan sighed. She loved her mom. But Jordan didn't know how to react to her mom's special talent for spoiling good things, even if she didn't mean to.

"Your friends at school must be impressed," said her dad as he took a sip of his coffee.

Jordan shrugged. "I guess."

He squinted one eye at Jordan. It was his way of saying that nothing got past him. "What's wrong?"

Jordan tried to change the subject. "Are you coming in to watch the Phoenix game with me, Dad?"

"First things first." He motioned for her to sit. "What's going on?"

Jordan sat on the corner of the coffee table. How could she tell them? It was humiliating. She wanted her parents to think she was popular at school. She couldn't admit that things weren't great. Besides, what could they do about it?

"Did something happen?" her dad asked.

Jordan stared at an old carpet stain. "Just some name-calling. No big deal."

Jordan's mom turned off the TV. "What kinds of names?" she asked.

"Jock."

"Oh." Her mom made it sound as if it were no big deal.

"You shouldn't let that bother you," said her dad. He reclined his chair back and the leg rest popped up loudly.

"Your dad's right," her mom said. "You know what a jock is?"

"Somebody who's into sports." Jordan played with a chip in her fingernail.

"A jock is an athlete," her mom said. "And you're an athlete."

It isn't what they say, but how they say it, Jordan thought. *Like they have a bad taste in their mouths.* But how could she make her mom understand that?

"Maybe they mean it as a compliment," her mom suggested.

Her dad shook his head. "They don't mean it as a compliment, Lois."

Jordan felt a lump in her throat. She knew her dad was right. Why was she being singled out? There were other girls on the basketball team who were just as athletic. Like Hazel, who was into basketball as much as Jordan. Well, maybe not quite as much, but close enough. And Hazel wasn't getting picked on.

"What did I tell you?" asked her mom. "Boys don't like girls to be better than them at sports."

"That shouldn't matter," said her dad. He shook his head at her mom.

"But you know it does," her mom said.

Jordan's phone buzzed with a text message, but she didn't bother to look.

"Hazel beats the boys on the reserve sometimes," Jordan said. "They've got an outdoor court there and she says they play every night, even when it's raining. Sometimes she's the only girl. And sometimes she plays against older boys — much older. That's how she got so good. And nobody bugs *her* about it."

Her mom leaned forward. "It could be because boys don't like loud girls, either."

Jordan flashed her mom an annoyed look. "I'm not loud."

"Remember that game I came to watch?" her mom said. "I saw how you shouted out those plays on the court and pointed to where players should go. Boys don't like girls taking charge like that. Maybe that's why they're calling you names."

"You sound like you're on their side," Jordan snapped.

"No, not at all," said her mom. "I'm not saying it's right. I'm just saying that that's the way the world seems to work. Honestly, I think it stinks."

Jordan stood up. "My game's starting. My NRWNBA game. Not Really Women National Basketball Association."

"Your what?" asked her dad.

"Never mind," said Jordan.

She left the room before her parents could say another word. From the hall closet, she grabbed her basketball before she nestled under her fuzzy blanket. She put the basketball next to her and rested her hand on the little bumps of rubber. It soothed her, the only thing that made her feel sure of herself.

Jordan turned up the volume on the TV and watched the Phoenix Mercury guard dribble up the court. The player fed the ball down low to her teammate, who then sunk a quick hook shot.

Jordan cheered under her breath. Then she remembered that her phone had buzzed. Probably Samira. Jordan touched the screen. To her surprise, it was a text from Amin. She'd never got a text from Amin before. She didn't even know how he got her number.

Are you watching the Phoenix game?

Yes.

Me too. Maybe we could watch it together?

Jordan caught her breath. On TV, the Minnesota Lynx took the lead by four points. She paused for several moments before starting to type her answer.

Sure. Do you want to come over here?

Jordan waited. She felt nervous to hit SEND. Normally, she wouldn't be worried about inviting a boy over to her house. From all her years of playing sports, her parents were used to her having boys over to hang out. But Amin was different. She didn't know what to expect if Amin came over.

She hit SEND.

Amin responded instantly.

Be there in ten minutes.

9 MUSCLES

Amin showed up during the second quarter. Smiling, he handed Jordan a paper bag. It was the program from a Phoenix Mercury game, plus a Phoenix Mercury banner.

"Wow, thanks!" Jordan said.

"My mom saw them play last year," Amin said. "She was in Phoenix on a business trip during the play-offs. She said it was amazing to see them play in real life. It was against Seattle. My mom is looking forward to meeting you. She thinks it's awesome that you're a big fan of Taurasi. That's her favourite player."

Jordan could hardly believe her ears. The Phoenix Mercury in real life! On top of that, Amin seemed excited about women's basketball. "Nobody I know watches the WNBA," she said.

"It's not big around here," Amin agreed. "But at home we never miss a game."

"You and your mom?" Jordan asked.

"And my sister, when she's home from university.

She's a point guard on the University of British Columbia team."

"UBC? Really?" Jordan blurted.

"Really," Amin laughed.

"My older brother is in university, too. SFU," Jordan said. "But he's not playing any sports there. He used to play football in high school. He wasn't very good."

"Well, my sister is good," Amin said. He nodded at the TV. "The Mercury had a hard time shutting down the Lynx last time they played them." He sat down on the couch next to Jordan with the bowl of popcorn between them. "Wonder how it'll go today."

"Hard to say. It's anybody's game —"

On the TV, a Mercury forward sank a jumper under pressure.

"What a shot she's got," said Amin. "I wish I could play like that."

"Me too," Jordan said.

"Wouldn't mind being in good shape like that, either," Amin said. "Look at how muscly their arms are, almost like a guy's."

Did he mean that as a good thing or an insult? Jordan wondered. She took a quick glimpse of his face but she couldn't tell.

He was right, though. The players arms were lean and wiry, their legs strong as they cut sharply around the court. They looked confident as they powered through the play.

"I love the Mercury's uniforms," Jordan said.

"Aren't you guys getting new uniforms for next game? I bet you're excited." Amin grabbed a handful of popcorn. "I swear I started playing better when we got our new uniforms."

Jordan thought of the stupid uniforms she'd have to start wearing at the next game. They were nothing like the pro women's uniforms, loose and athletic. What was her team thinking? That only men should wear *real* basketball uniforms? That only men play *real* basketball?

During the break, an ad for women's deodorant came on. The voice told the women, "Never let them see you sweat." There were images of women with their arms in the air, their armpits dry as a desert. Even the woman sprinting down the road didn't sweat a bead.

"So dumb," Amin said. "You should see how much my sister sweats during her basketball games. She's a real jock."

Jordan flinched at the sound of the word. *Jock*. Amin used it like it was nothing. He'd heard his teammates calling her Jordan the Jock, he must have. Didn't he know how much it embarrassed her?

"Whoa, look at that move!" Amin exclaimed. He pointed at the TV. "Watch the replay!"

Jordan tried to forget about what he had said. "That move was awesome," she agreed.

At half-time, a woman with a microphone interviewed two of the Mercury players. They talked about what had changed since last year, why their game was so much better. They talked about the conditioning they'd done pre-season and how weightlifting had propelled them to another level. Their hard, cut arms glistened with sweat.

"My team needs better conditioning," Jordan said. She thought of how exhausted the Orcas were during the game against the Mavericks.

"For sure," Amin said. "If you want to be a serious athlete, you have to do a lot of conditioning. Both cardio and strength."

Jordan had seen the boys' team in the school's weightlifting room. She wondered why the girls only ever ran lines at the start of practice. "Maybe I'll ask Coach Banford to book the weightlifting room once a week for us," she said.

"You'll get all muscly like the Mercury players," Amin said. "My sister lifts weights. She's an amazing athlete. Her fitness level is crazy good."

Jordan couldn't make sense of Amin. On one hand, he seemed to be saying that Jordan would get muscly in a bad way. On the other hand, he claimed that serious athletes should lift weights. And he lit up with pride every time he mentioned his sister.

"If you're going to lift weights, you have to do it more often than once a week at school," Amin advised.

"Do you have any weights here?"

"My mom has a set of weights in the garage. She bought them years ago and only ever used them once."

"I could find out what weightlifting program my sister does and tell you," Amin offered.

"That would be great," said Jordan. But she knew she wouldn't wait that long. She could research this herself. She could find out what the Phoenix Mercury players did and copy that.

After the game was over and Amin had left, Jordan wasted no time. In the garage, she found her mom's dumbbells in the corner, covered with cobwebs. She dusted them off and looked at the list of exercises she'd found online. She guessed at starting weights and then did her first routine.

She did lunges first, followed by a *clean and press*, lifting the dumbbells from the floor all the way over her head in one motion. She did arm curls and triceps presses and more lunges until she was exhausted. She collapsed in a sweating heap on the garage floor.

10 Serious ATHLETES

"The new uniforms are here," Samira announced. "Just in time for our game!" She burst into the change room with a large cardboard box in her arms.

Jordan stayed on the bench. The rest of the team rushed to the box and helped Samira to tear the flaps open. The girls rummaged through the uniforms, each looking for their jersey number.

"They're so fancy!" Tara said. "Even the shorts have our numbers on the bottom corner!"

"Here are yours, Jordan." Mayleen tossed her two pairs of shorts and two jerseys — a white one for home games and a blue one for away games.

Before changing into the new uniform, Jordan held the jersey in her outstretched arms. It looked too small. The tiny sleeves were the size of grapefruit wedges, and when she slipped the shirt over her head, the sides fit snug against her ribs.

"You look so good!" Petra told Samira.

"The shorts are super cute!" Samira said, turning to

check herself out in the mirror. "We all look great!"

"We all look like we're going to the mall," Jordan said under her breath. "Not playing a basketball game."

On the bench next to Jordan, Hazel whispered, "I'm with you. These are stupid."

Inside a bathroom stall where nobody could see her, Jordan stuck her knee into the front of her jersey and stretched it out. She grasped the sides of her shorts and pulled at them, too. But they just snapped back into their original form. With a groan, Jordan gave up and left the change room. She headed out to the gym, leaving the rest of her team to finish fixing their hair at the mirror. Lately, they seemed to be taking longer to get ready for a game, fussing over how they looked.

In the gym, Jordan took a few shots from in close to warm up. Although the new jersey stretched with her body, she felt like it was restricting the movement of her shot. She tried to put it out of her mind, but she felt really uncomfortable in the new uniform. It was designed to draw attention to her body. All she wanted people to notice was her dribbling and her passing and her three-point shot.

"Honestly," Hazel said as she walked onto the court. She was pulling at her jersey. "I feel pretty mad at the team right now."

"Me too," Jordan said. "But we can't let it get to us. We have a game to play." The game was against the Fleetwood Arrows.

"What does Fleetwood put in their water?" Hazel asked Jordan. "They're giants."

They watched Fleetwood warm up at the other end of the court. Jordan saw that Hazel was right. The Arrows had several players who were very tall. They made Hazel, who was the Orcas' tallest player, look tiny in comparison.

"We'll just have to block them out," Jordan said. Then she called out to her team, "Line up for lay-ups! Two lines — shooting side and rebound side."

Jordan dribbled to the hoop. She banked the ball off the backboard and into the net. From the rebound side, Samira came across at the same time and grabbed the ball. Something sparkly caught Jordan's eye.

Jordan ran over to Samira's spot in the shooting line. "You can't wear those earrings in the game," she said.

Samira touched her earlobes. "But they're not hoops or anything. They're just little studs."

"You know the rules," Jordan said. "The ref will make you take them off."

Samira checked the bleachers. Wyatt, Amin and some of their teammates were perched in the top corner. Samira rolled her eyes and marched off to the change room to put away her earrings.

The height of the Fleetwood team proved to be a bigger challenge than Jordan had thought. The problem was that they weren't only tall, but were excellent rebounders, too. The Orcas quickly found themselves down by ten points.

At the start of the second quarter, Jordan dribbled the ball up the court. She passed to Mayleen, who made a spin move on her defender. From the top of the key, Mayleen pulled up a shot. But she must have missed Number 8 coming across the paint. With a thunderous *boom!* Number 8 blocked Mayleen's shot, sending the ball flying down the court and out of bounds.

Jordan raced to get the ball from the ref.

"Stack three!" she called.

Hazel and Mayleen hustled into position. Jogging behind them, Petra joined the line.

"Samira, let's go, let's go!" Hazel shouted.

Jordan couldn't believe it. Samira was *walking* to join the stack. She was wasting time fixing her ponytail.

Jordan called out, "Hustle, Samira!"

It was too late. The Fleetwood team had enough time to read the stack. As the Orcas cut in different directions, the Fleetwood defence stuck with them. Jordan could find no one open. Finally, she forced a pass to Petra. But it was intercepted by the Arrows' Number 14, who lobbed a long ball to Number 8 for a breakaway and an easy basket.

"We have to start out-muscling them in the paint," Jordan told Samira at half-time.

"They're too strong," Samira said. She sounded

distracted. She stared across the court at the bleachers where the boys sat in their uniforms.

"You just need to force your way to the inside," Jordan told her. "Get your hips against their bodies."

Samira nodded and smoothed out the front of her jersey. She wiped away small smudges of eyeliner from under her eyes.

The second half didn't go any better for the Orcas. The score was 44–32 for the Arrows going into the fourth quarter. Hazel had given it her all under the net, but it had cost her three personal fouls.

Jordan brought the ball up the court and signaled to Samira for a pick. Samira cut toward Jordan and set a screen behind Jordan's check, Number 9. Exploding into a full sprint, Jordan dribbled the ball around Samira. But Samira had set the screen too far away from Jordan's defender. Number 9 skirted Samira and poked the ball from Jordan.

"Grab it, Samira!" Jordan yelled. She scrambled for the ball as it bounced past Samira.

Samira took a couple of steps toward the ball, but she didn't bend over to grab it. Number 9 reached it first. She held on to the ball to settle down the play and let her team get a head start up the court.

Jordan clenched her jaw. Her team was playing a terrible game.

At the final buzzer, the score was 60–42.

Before heading to the change room, Jordan took

her water bottle to the other end of the bench where Samira was sitting. She wanted to ask Samira why she hadn't tried as hard as usual. She remembered their last game against the Elgin Eagles. That was when Jordan had first noticed something different about the way Samira was moving on the court. Samira wasn't acting like the player she used to be.

"Think Wyatt likes the new uniforms?" Samira asked.

"How should I know?" Jordan snapped. "All I know is that I don't like the new uniforms. They're stupid."

Samira frowned.

"I wish we'd picked real basketball uniforms," Jordan continued. "We should've taken it more seriously."

Samira put her hand on her hip. "Oh, I see. We're only serious athletes if we dress the way you want?"

"No," Jordan fumbled for words. "I didn't mean —"

She didn't have a chance to finish her sentence. Abruptly, Samira turned away and said something to Mayleen. Then she hurried off to the change room.

Jordan found herself alone at the bench.

"Look," said a voice. It was Wyatt and Leo. "It's Amin's girlfriend, the jock," said Wyatt as they both threw their bags onto the floor.

Jordan's chest tightened. She turned away from Wyatt.

"I wonder," Wyatt said. "I mean, it *seems* like she's

his girlfriend. But is that even possible? Do jocks have boyfriends, Leo?"

"I've heard that girls like Jordan don't even like boys," Leo said.

"It's true." Wyatt nodded smugly. "All female jocks are gay. That's a fact."

"Leave me alone," Jordan said, grabbing her duffel bag.

Wyatt laughed. "Jordan the Jock must be eager to get to the girls' change room."

Jordan sped around the corner. She almost crashed into Ms. Murray, the school counsellor. "Sorry," Jordan muttered.

As she hurried down the hallway, Jordan could hear Wyatt call out loudly from the gym, "There's no shame in being gay, Jordan!"

11 ALLIANCE

As Jordan walked into Science class the following week, Amin rushed up to her.

"Want to be lab partners today?" he asked. He seemed to be out of breath.

"Okay." Jordan grinned.

Amin turned sideways to let some kids make their way to their desks. "Chemical and physical properties of metals. Going to be exciting stuff."

"Doesn't sound very exciting," Jordan said.

"Not at all," Amin agreed.

They put on their white lab coats and safety goggles. Then they got their materials set up at the counter.

"I'll test the metals and you record the results," Jordan said. Then she remembered what her mom had said about girls taking charge. "Unless you want to test the metals?"

Amin shook his head. "You start. We can take turns."

Jordan pressed a magnet against a square of aluminum.

"Not magnetic," she reported to Amin.

As Amin recorded the information on the lab sheet, Jordan stared at the soft curl of dark hair that hooked around his ear. Did he know that she liked him? Did he like her? It seemed as though he did, but she wasn't sure.

Around the class, pairs of students leaned over their lab materials and talked quietly to each other as they worked. Jordan used to think that when the whole class wore lab coats and safety glasses, they all looked exactly alike. But this time, Jordan noticed that the girls somehow managed to look cute, while she looked plain and sloppy and — *Not feminine*, she thought.

After the lab was finished, Jordan went back to her own seat to write up the results on a worksheet. She saw that she had mixed up the metals in her description. So she crumpled the worksheet and tried to toss it in the garbage can from her desk. It missed. She went to pick it up off the floor.

A boy named Mark said, "Jordan the Jock misses the net." He mimicked the tone of a TV sports commentator.

Jordan froze on the spot. The nickname was spreading beyond the basketball court. She looked across the room to where Amin sat at his desk and was relieved to see him hunched over his paper. Amin hadn't heard Mark. Jordan went to the counter and took a fresh worksheet from the pile.

When the bell rang for the next class, Jordan wove through the crowded hall toward her locker. As she passed one of the small counselling offices, Ms. Murray called out to her through the open door.

"Tough game last week," Ms. Murray said. "I only caught the last bit of it. Those Fleetwood players were giant."

Jordan stepped inside the office. "They outpowered us under the net."

"Even Hazel had a hard time rebounding," Ms. Murray agreed. Then she raised an eyebrow at Jordan. "I see you have new uniforms."

Jordan sighed. "I hate them. I voted for different ones."

Ms. Murray nodded. "I would imagine so."

Why? Jordan wondered. *Because I'm not feminine enough for those uniforms?*

"You obviously take basketball very seriously, Jordan." Ms. Murray opened the top drawer of her desk. "You're a very good player. Do you plan to play university ball?"

Jordan shrugged.

After rummaging around in the drawer, Ms. Murray finally pulled out a few pamphlets and stared at them as she spoke. "If you have a dream in life, you can't be afraid to say it to people. When I was in high school, I wanted more than anything to play varsity badminton. I told everybody that I was going to make the team."

"Did you?"

"You bet I did," said Ms. Murray, looking up from the pamphlets. "Badminton. Now *there's* a sport a lot of people don't take seriously — whether you're a woman or a man. But at the top level? Badminton is a tough, fast sport, let me tell you."

Jordan nodded. "I do want to play university ball."

Ms. Murray smiled. "Good."

"Maybe even the WNBA someday," Jordan added shyly.

"Well, you're only in grade nine, so it's early still. But starting next year, I can help make sure you've got the right courses to get into university. And at some point, we can check out athletic scholarships together."

Jordan's stomach swirled with excitement.

"It's never too early to start preparing for scholarships. You might want to consider getting involved in a few more school activities. Serving your school looks good on applications. Something like this, for example."

Ms. Murray handed a pamphlet to Jordan. On the front it read:

White Rock Junior High School Green Club.

"If you're concerned about the planet, this group of students does a lot of good projects around the school," Ms. Murray explained. She handed Jordan a second pamphlet. "Or there's this one. If you like a good debate."

White Rock High School Debating Club.

"Or —" Ms. Murray paused and looked at Jordan. "There's this one."

White Rock High School GSA. Gay-Straight Alliance.

"The Gay-Straight Alliance is a group of students who work to create safe spaces for LGBTQ students in our school," Ms. Murray explained. "It's a very important group and they welcome anybody. You might find it helpful."

"Thanks." Jordan folded the pamphlets and stuffed them in her jeans pocket.

"By the way," Ms. Murray said as Jordan was heading out the door. "I wouldn't have voted for those uniforms either."

★★★

That night, Jordan pulled the pamphlets out of her pocket. She spread them flat on the desk in her bedroom. Her attention kept going to one. *White Rock High School GSA. Gay-Straight Alliance.*

Jordan remembered how Wyatt had accused her of being gay — as if it was a terrible thing. She looked at the WNBA posters on her walls. She could name every player and every statistic about them. She didn't know which ones were gay, except that Diana Taurasi had married a teammate.

What did it matter, anyway? It didn't.

Did Ms. Murray think Jordan liked girls? Maybe Ms. Murray heard Wyatt from the hallway after the basketball game and was trying to help Jordan — just in case. Was that really why Ms. Murray had given Jordan the pamphlet? Or was she just urging Jordan to get more involved in school activities, like she'd said? After all, she'd also given Jordan pamphlets on the environment and debating clubs. Plus, the *GSA* wasn't just for LGBTQ students. It was also for students who wanted to support their LGBTQ classmates.

Am I getting too paranoid about what people think of me? Jordan thought.

It was hard not to, thanks to Wyatt. Wyatt was right about one thing, though, even if he had said it sarcastically: There was no shame in being gay.

Only Jordan wasn't. And she was tired of Wyatt and his friends deciding who and what she was. She crumpled the *GSA* pamphlet and tossed it into the bin next to her desk.

12 Everything is DIFFERENT

Jordan stood on the court and waited for Coach Banford to start practice. Around her, the rest of the team took shots from various spots on the floor. More than anything, Jordan loved being on a gym court. It was the one thing that could make her forget about everything else.

The practice started with running lines. Even though Jordan's legs were tight and sore from her morning routine of lifting weights in her garage, she pushed harder than usual. The last game hadn't gone well. But Jordan was still pumped from her 21-point game against the Eagles. And she wanted to stay at the top of the league for scoring.

"Rebound practice today," Coach Banford said. "We've been a little weak under the net the past two games."

The girls stood in two lines along the edges of the key. Coach Banford alternated which sides of the back-board he threw the ball toward. When it was Jordan's turn, she jumped as high as she could, arms stretched up high. She tried to time the rebound perfectly. As always, she practised as if she were in a game, conjuring up images in her head of exciting action. She caught the ball and pivoted away from an imaginary defence.

"Chin the ball!" Coach Banford called out. To demonstrate, he held a ball under his chin with a tight grip, his elbows sticking out far to the sides.

Jordan nodded and jogged to the back of the line behind Samira. "We should practice rebounds."

Samira chuckled. "We *are* practising rebounds."

"At my house, I mean. Did you see my rebound? It was terrible."

"You're a guard. You rebound the ball maybe twice a game, if that." Samira moved up as the line shifted forward.

Both of them stopped talking to watch Hazel, the best rebounder on the team. Hazel's timing seemed perfect. Taking a step toward the net, she drove her knee toward the ceiling and leaped up. Her feet rose several inches off the floor. She snatched the ball hard out of the air, her body arched back. Like a cat she landed with barely a sound. She crouched low. Chinning the ball exactly as Coach Banford had shown them, she pivoted wildly back and forth, pretending to look for an outlet pass.

During the water break, Jordan talked to Hazel about her vertical, the distance she could jump off the ground. "How do you jump so high?" Jordan asked. "Your vertical must be almost a foot."

"Actually," Hazel smiled, "it's fourteen inches. My dad measures it every week for me. Last week it increased a whole inch."

"You're so lucky," Jordan said.

Wiping the sweat from her neck with a towel, Hazel shook her head. "Not luck. It's the skipping program I'm doing."

Samira turned. "I used to love skipping when I was little."

"This is a bit different," explained Hazel. "Part of it is just regular skipping. But then you increase how many double and triple spins of the rope you can do."

"That sounds too hard for me," said Samira.

"It's based on how Japanese samurai trained," Hazel explained. "They'd jump over fields of wheat or something. As the wheat grew taller and taller, they'd slowly be able to jump higher and higher."

Jordan wondered how long it took for the skipping program to work. She didn't want to wait for wheat to grow. Maybe she could increase her vertical by the time they played the Mavericks again. "I bet Coach Banford will let me borrow a skipping rope from the equipment room. I'll add some samurai training to my weightlifting," Jordan said.

"You're weightlifting?" Samira asked.

Coach Banford blew his whistle. "Back to it, team!"

"Jordan, what are you doing that for?" Samira persisted. She shook her head.

"I'll play better if I'm fit," Jordan replied.

The girls headed to the other end of the court. Coach Banford was setting up orange cones for a drill.

"Skipping, I get," Samira said. "But weightlifting? You've seen those women on the muscle magazines, right?"

Jordan pictured the magazines she'd seen at the grocery store. Women in bathing suits with dark tans and oiled skin, flexing their muscles at bodybuilding competitions.

"Aren't you worried you'll get too big?" Samira asked.

Samira's question pricked at Jordan. She thought of what the boys had said about the photos in her locker. How the women basketball players looked like men.

"One-on-one defensive drill," Coach Banford announced. "I want the dribblers to hold their heads up. No looking down at the ball. Defence, you sit low in the crouch, one hand high to block a pass, one hand low. Mirror that ball."

Because Samira and Jordan were already standing next to each other, they paired up. Jordan started on offence. Her aim was to beat the defence to each cone all the way down the court.

Jordan headed toward the first cone, dribbling the ball low at her side. She bent her other arm out in front of her for better ball protection and faked a cross-over. Then she pulled the ball back and exploded past Samira. When Jordan reached the first cone, Samira jogged to catch up and set up in the defensive stance again.

"Crouch low, Samira!" yelled Coach Banford.

But Samira didn't crouch as low as she usually did. Instead, she stood almost upright. She shuffled her feet only a little in order to keep Jordan from beating her to the next cone. Jordan pulled the ball behind her back and exploded past Samira again. Jordan had to wait at the next cone for Samira as this time she walked to catch up.

"You're hardly trying," Jordan said.

"I *am* trying," Samira said.

"It doesn't seem like it."

Jordan started toward the last cone. She made a head fake, then crossed the ball over to her left hand. Jordan was one of the only players on the Orcas who could dribble just as strongly with both her left and right hands. She faked one more time before using her new spin move.

Samira swatted at the ball but hit Jordan's arm.

"Foul," Jordan said as she sprinted to the cone. "You should shuffle diagonally to cut me off instead of just swinging for the ball."

"Sorry I'm not as good as you," Samira said.

Jordan detected sarcasm. "I never said that."

"Sure." Samira started toward the bench.

"What's the matter with you?" Jordan asked.

"Nothing." Samira turned and frowned at Jordan. "Not everybody takes basketball as seriously as you. Did you ever think of that?"

"You seem to be holding back lately." Jordan turned to watch the play on the court.

Samira didn't reply right away. Finally, she shrugged and said, "I guess I just haven't felt like it."

"Haven't felt like it?"

"Things change, Jordan," Samira said.

"What things?"

"I'm not sure I want to play basketball anymore."

"What?" Jordan was shocked. "You can't quit."

"I haven't said I'm quitting for sure," Samira said. "I'm thinking about it."

Jordan felt as though she'd been punched in the stomach. "What about your commitment to the team?"

"I know." Samira sounded ashamed of herself. "But I really like Wyatt."

"So? What does that have to do with it?"

Samira stared at the floor.

"Really, Samira?" Jordan raised her voice. "You're going to quit basketball because of him? You love basketball."

"High school makes things different," Samira said.

"High school doesn't make things different. *You're* making things different," Jordan said. But even as she said it, she didn't quite believe it.

"Aren't you worried?" Samira asked.

"About what?"

"Amin," Samira said. "Aren't you worried that he might not like a girl who's too athletic?"

"No," Jordan said. But it was a lie, and she knew it.

13 BULLYING

Jordan hit the SNOOZE button the next morning. Her heart wasn't into getting up early to weightlift. In fact, she wasn't sure she'd ever lift weights again. She was fed up with hearing what everyone thought. And after the argument with Samira at the end of practice, Jordan had forgotten to borrow a skipping rope from the equipment room.

Today was the Orcas' last home game before the big rematch against the Marriott Mavericks. On the day of the rematch, the teachers were going to let students miss an afternoon class to have a big pep rally. Jordan wasn't quite sure what happened at a pep rally, but it sounded exciting.

Before the game against the Newton Rockets, Jordan checked the league website on her phone. Number 10 on the Mavericks, a player named Shawna Yee, was now in the top scorer position. She was ahead of Jordan by six points. The Newton Rockets were in the middle of the standings — not very good, but not bad either. Jordan might have a chance to get a few points out of the game.

At the start of the game, Hazel won the tipoff, sending the ball straight into Jordan's hands. Dribbling the ball up court, Jordan called, "Triangle!" and headed to the outside of the three-point line. Her defender maintained a safe yet close distance. Jordan considered taking a shot. But Mayleen's defender was out of position in the triangle, so Jordan lobbed a soft pass over everyone's head. Mayleen read it perfectly and scored the first two points of the game.

Rockets Number 5 brought the ball across the centre line and held up two fingers to call the play. Samira checked Number 5, mirroring her zigzags on the court. Suddenly Number 5 blasted past Samira, going deep into the paint. Hazel had no choice but to come across the paint, dropping her own check, to stop Number 5 from making an easy lay-up. Number 5 spotted the opening and bounce passed it under Hazel's arm to her open teammate. Two points Rockets.

Back and forth it went for the entire first half. Mayleen's check kept lagging behind the play. So, instead of shooting, Jordan kept passing the ball to Mayleen. In fact, Jordan hadn't taken a single shot. With all Mayleen's points, they should have been winning easily. But Rockets Number 5 was scoring as often as Mayleen. Jordan figured Number 5 had scored most of the Rockets' points.

Whenever Number 5 came down the court with the ball, Jordan could tell she was just waiting for Samira to ease off on defence. And Samira did, every single time. Jordan was getting frustrated with Samira. Just like at practice, it seemed that she wasn't even trying. Twice Jordan caught Samira checking out the boys' team in the bleachers.

Coach Banford noticed it, too. "Stick with her, Samira! Focus!"

But it didn't work. Samira kept playing in the same half-hearted way. She carried herself on the court in a way that was unlike the old Samira Jordan had known since primary grades. In the past, Samira had always moved in a casual, playful way. Now she acted as if — Jordan couldn't put her finger on it — as if Samira thought she was being watched all the time.

As if she's posing for a camera, Jordan thought.

"What do you think about switching checks with me?" Jordan asked Samira at half-time.

"What do you think about passing a little more?" Samira snapped.

"I *am* passing."

"To Mayleen," Samira said.

"You're never open."

Jordan wanted to add, *You aren't even trying to get open*. But she bit her tongue and walked away. She tried to wrap her mind around the second half.

But the second half didn't go any better. Samira

put more effort into her defence, but not much more. Several times Jordan caught her checking the bleachers where Wyatt was sitting with his team.

With three minutes left in the game, Number 5 passed the ball to the other guard. Then she sprinted down the sidelines, along the baseline, and back around to receive a pass back. Samira trailed far behind her, jogging at half the speed. She left Number 5 free to sink an outside shot with no pressure.

When the ref handed the ball to Jordan behind the baseline, Jordan smacked it hard in frustration. She shook her head at Samira. Before passing the ball inbounds to her, Jordan muttered under her breath, "Maybe you *should* just quit."

Samira didn't say anything. If she heard Jordan, she acted like she hadn't.

After the Orcas lost the game by four points, Jordan left before the boys' game started. As she headed out of the gym, she spotted Samira sitting with Tara and Petra in the bleachers to cheer the boys on. Amin took shots on the court. Jordan caught his eye, and he gave her a small wave.

Alone, Jordan headed home, taking the usual route past the park and down along the row of small stores. When she turned the corner, she spotted a group of kids from the school heading toward her. Jordan guessed they were on their way to see the boys' team play. She knew a couple of the kids — one was that friend of

Wyatt's from science class. Mark, the one who called her Jordan the Jock when she missed the garbage can.

Jordan's stomach tightened. Would he say something about her? To her? She didn't want to take the chance. The thought of being teased almost brought tears to her eyes.

Quickly, Jordan darted behind a tall hedge in front of a small house. She could hear the voices slowly getting closer. She held her breath.

Maybe this is a dumb idea, she thought. *The only thing more embarrassing than being teased would be to get caught hiding behind someone's hedges.*

In the window of the small house, an old lady sat in a chair. She gave Jordan a puzzled look. Jordan waved shyly. She was relieved when the lady waved back without getting up from her chair.

The voices were loud now. The kids talked about going to the movies Friday night. They laughed at a story one of them told about their little sister stuffing plastic beads up her nose. It didn't sound like a funny story to Jordan. The doctor had to remove the beads with special pliers.

As Jordan waited quietly, a thought struck her. She'd never been really popular in school, but she had always had plenty of friends. For the most part, she had got along with everyone. Never in a million years would Jordan have thought that she'd be bullied like this.

But is it bullying or are they just teasing me? she wondered.

The year before, on Pink Shirt Day, her math teacher Mr. Perez had explained the difference. "Teasing," he said, "can be a way of connecting with another person. Like if you say to your friend after they miss the hoop, 'Nice shot, Kobe Bryant.' It can also be a way to kindly change your friend's mind. Like if you say, 'Hey, sleepyhead, why don't you pick up your pencil and actually do a math question?' But bullying," he went on, his voice turning very serious, "is meant to hurt. It's meant to embarrass."

After the kids passed the hedge, Jordan waited a few minutes before stepping out onto the sidewalk. By the time Jordan finally emerged from the hedge, the other kids were small dots far up the road.

14 BLOCKED OUT

For the next week, Jordan and Samira didn't talk much. Sure, they chatted at their lockers between classes. Mostly to complain about homework or to report something funny somebody said in their class. But it wasn't the same. Samira hadn't come to Jordan's house to hang out at all. Jordan could feel that something had changed between them. She regretted what she'd said to Samira during the last game. That she thought Samira should quit. It was an awful thing to say, and also untrue.

Jordan didn't think Samira should quit. She didn't want Samira to quit. She wanted things back to what they were before.

But there was one thing that kept Jordan hopeful. Samira was still showing up for basketball. She'd changed her mind about quitting. Or maybe she had decided to at least finish the season.

At practice after school, Coach Banford warned the team he was going to push them hard. "One more week until the big rematch. Still have to work on our rebounds. Plus our defensive footwork."

On the court next to the girls, the boys' team ran through a series of dribbling manoeuvres. Through the circle of girls, Jordan watched Amin sprint full-speed between the cones. In front of Amin, Wyatt finished his drill and then looked over at the girls' team. He nodded at Samira and wiggled his eyebrows. It was as if he was saying that she should be impressed by him. Samira's face flushed and she smiled at him.

"Three sets of lines — let's go!" Coach Banford said, clapping his hands.

The girls lined up on the baseline. They sprinted to touch each line on the gym floor, back to the baseline and then onto the next line. It was tiring to bend over and touch each line, especially after running as hard as they could. Jordan was not that fast compared to the others — Tara was a cheetah and Hazel ran like a gazelle.

When it came time to work on rebounds, Coach Banford paired them up by height. Jordan was paired with Samira.

"This drill is going to get messy," Coach Banford explained. "I want everyone to move into the key as soon as I put up the shot. It'll be crowded. Just focus on blocking out your check."

Everyone got ready, eagerly waiting for Coach Banford's shot. When it went up, all the players jostled hard to get a step on their check and block them out with their hips. Jordan managed easily to get the inside position on Samira. Hazel snagged the rebound and tossed it back to Coach Banford.

The second time the ball went up, Jordan moved once again into the inside position. She bumped Samira hard in the thigh with her hip.

"Ouch," Samira said and staggered backward.

Jordan looked back but didn't say a word.

"You don't have to be so rough," Samira said.

"It's how you're supposed to do it," Jordan huffed.

Over on the next court, the boys were taking a water break. Some of them were walking past the girls' court to go for a bathroom break.

Coach Banford released the third shot. Then he walked away to the equipment room to get something, leaving the girls on their own.

This time, Jordan's play was even more physical. She planted her hip against Samira. As the others scrambled for the rebound, Jordan leaned harder and harder against Samira, keeping her elbows out wide.

Mayleen almost grabbed the rebound, but the ball popped loose in the air. Some of the girls let out quiet grunts of exertion as they jostled and stretched for the ball.

"Oh! Get it, get it," Wyatt called as he walked behind the baseline. "Block them out!"

Samira whispered in Jordan's ear, "Calm down!"

But Jordan kept leaning against Samira, pushing her out of range of the rebound.

Suddenly Samira backed off, sending Jordan crashing to the floor. Tara grabbed the rebound and the play stopped.

"I told you to calm down," Samira said, looking at Jordan. Then she turned to Wyatt and rolled her eyes. "Jordan the Jock."

Wyatt laughed.

Jordan climbed to her feet. She glared at Samira.

The other girls must have sensed the tension. They stood frozen, waiting. In the back corner, Coach Banford made clattering noises as he rummaged for something in the equipment room.

Then Wyatt, still standing behind the hoop, started laughing even harder.

Jordan's face turned hot. She couldn't take the laughing. Something inside her snapped. Without thinking, she shoved Samira with all her might.

Samira fell hard onto the floor. Wincing in pain, she clutched the back of her head. Tara and Hazel rushed to her.

Wyatt narrowed his eyes and shook his head at Jordan. "What's your problem?"

"Jordan."

It was Coach Banford. His voice was stern.

She turned to see him at centre court. He motioned for her to join him there.

"What just happened?" he asked.

Jordan bit the inside of her lip to keep from crying.

She knew that Coach Banford hadn't heard what Samira had said. And she wasn't about to explain it to him. It was too embarrassing to tell her side of the story.

"This behaviour —" He paused, then sighed. "This is not the sort of leadership I expect from my captain. And this is certainly not the sort of leadership you're capable of."

Jordan nodded. Without a word, she started to walk out of the gym. She could feel all eyes on her. Coach Banford called her back, but Jordan just kept walking.

For the first time in her life, Jordan felt like she hated basketball. In her heart she knew that wasn't true. She knew there was no place better than a basketball court. But she was going to have to convince herself otherwise.

★★★

That night, Jordan made a decision.

I am quitting basketball, she thought.

In her bedroom, she pulled down the posters of Diana Taurasi and other WNBA players. On her desk, her phone buzzed with a text, but she didn't feel like talking to anybody. She shut off her phone without checking the message. Then she pulled down the Phoenix Mercury banner Amin's mom had given her. She took the new uniforms, both home and away, out of her duffel bag.

She shoved it all under her bed.

15 Calling it QUITS

Jordan stood in front of her locker. Everything sounded far away to her. The kids laughing, the sneakers squeaking on the floor, the locker doors slamming. She could hear her heart beating in her ears as she took down her pictures of her basketball hero.

Hazel was putting away her binder two lockers down. "Big game next week, Jordan," she said. "I'm so ready for it, aren't you?"

Jordan swallowed hard. She knew what she'd decided. But saying it was different from taking magazine pictures off her locker door.

Jordan forced out the words. "I won't be playing."

"What?" Hazel's eyes went wide. "How come? Do you have an appointment or something? A family thing? Can't you get out of it?"

"I'm quitting the team."

"Are you sick?" asked Hazel.

Jordan shook her head.

"Don't tell me you're moving away."

"No, I just can't play anymore," Jordan said.

Hazel looked puzzled, like someone had told her the Earth was flat. "You have to play. We need you."

Jordan closed her locker.

"You're joking, right?"

Jordan looked straight at Hazel. "I'm not joking."

After Math class, Jordan had to walk all the way to the other end of the school for English. She felt like everyone was looking at her. A couple of times she was sure she heard her name and words like "basketball" and "quit" whispered as she went past. She didn't know that so many kids even knew she played on the team.

At lunch time, Mayleen and Petra were waiting for Jordan at her locker. A few classmates who weren't even on the basketball team joined them.

"Is it true?" Mayleen asked.

Jordan nodded.

Her friends surrounded her in a semi-circle as she spun the combination on her lock. It reminded Jordan of a nature movie she'd seen about wolves hunting a fawn.

Jordan was quitting to get *less* attention. And here she was getting even more of it.

"But why?" asked Petra.

"I just don't feel like playing anymore," Jordan replied.

"That's not a good reason," said Mayleen.

"I'm too busy with other stuff like homework."

"But you're our captain," Petra protested.

"Somebody else can be captain."

"We can get another captain. But who's going to lead us on the court like you do? Who else can get us to play like a team?" Mayleen was almost shouting.

Another classmate, a girl named Evelyn, piped up. "Jordan, you're the best player in our school. Everybody knows it. You can't quit. Especially not before the big rematch against the Mavericks."

"Sorry, guys," said Jordan. "My mind is made up."

"Fine. You go ahead and quit. But when we lose every game it'll be because of you." Angry, Petra turned down the hall.

Jordan felt a stab of guilt. She grabbed her lunch and walked slowly toward the cafeteria. From the door, she surveyed the room. She saw Samira, her back toward Jordan, sitting with Wyatt. They were both laughing as they ate their lunch. Normally, Samira would have lunch with Jordan and some of the other girls from the team. Today everyone was sitting apart.

Jordan walked to the corner and found a seat by herself. She pulled out her lunch and chewed her sandwich. It had no taste.

What would Samira say when she heard the news? Jordan had been really upset when Samira was thinking of quitting. She had questioned Samira's commitment to the team. And now here Jordan was, abandoning that same team.

When the bell rang at the end of the school day, Coach Banford approached Jordan in the hallway. "Jordan, if you have time, I'd like to talk to you about the next game after school."

"Uh, sure," Jordan mumbled.

Does he already know? she wondered. *I hope so. Then I won't have to tell him myself.*

She sat with Coach Banford in the small area outside the gym teacher's office. The gym teacher, Ms. Whiffle, was busy inside with paperwork.

"Jordan, I've heard a rumour," Coach Banford said. "Hard to imagine it's true. But if it is, I want to hear it from you."

"I was planning on telling you today," Jordan stumbled over her words.

"But why would you quit?"

"I have to spend more time on schoolwork."

"That is an important thing. But you seem to be doing well enough in all your classes."

Jordan looked toward the open office door. She couldn't tell him the real reason. He wouldn't understand and she wouldn't be able to explain her feelings to him. Not without bursting into tears, and that would humiliate her.

"Is it because of what happened at practice?" Coach Banford's voice was quiet, gentle.

"Maybe," Jordan said. It wasn't an outright lie, but it felt like one.

"If you apologize to Samira, we can put it behind us and you can still play," suggested Coach.

"No, I don't think so. I'm sorry, Coach."

"You are a valuable member of the team. And you're a strong captain. Your team counts on you," Coach Banford told her. "Don't forget that."

Jordan left the gym feeling even worse. She wanted to slink home and hide in her bedroom. Turning the corner, she bumped into Amin.

"You quit the team?" he asked.

"I don't really want to talk about it," Jordan said.

Amin nodded slowly. He looked like he was thinking carefully about something. "You never answered my text," he said.

"Oh, sorry," Jordan muttered. "I was busy. And then my battery died and I forgot to check it later."

"My sister's playing Sunday at UBC," Amin said. "I was wondering if you wanted to come with me to watch her. My dad can drive us."

Jordan thought about it for a moment. "Sure, I guess."

Amin smiled. "Then it's a date."

16 THUNDERBIRDS

After dinner on Sunday, Jordan stood at her closet deciding what to wear on her date with Amin. She'd never been on a date before. What do you wear to a basketball game? First, she picked a pair of jeans and a colourful T-shirt, but it seemed too plain. So she changed into black pants and a button-up shirt. Then she wondered if the plaid shirt made her look like Amin's buddy and not his date. Finally, she settled on a pair of grey jeans with a pink sweater.

In the bathroom, Jordan tried to use her mom's curling iron. She burned herself twice and decided the result made her look ridiculous. She put her hair up into a high ponytail. She worried that the ponytail made her look too much like she always did on the basketball court. She pulled out the elastic and used a hairclip instead. She put on some mascara.

Jordan sighed. Just then, she wished she'd said no to Amin. No matter what she did, Jordan worried that she didn't look "girly" enough.

She checked the time. Amin and his father would be there any minute to pick her up.

Jordan's heart sped up. She checked herself one last time in the mirror, took a deep breath and reminded herself that this was going to be fun. After all, she was getting to see an actual university basketball game. Despite everything that had happened lately, none of it changed how much she dreamed of playing university basketball.

"You look nice." Jordan's mom stood in the doorway.

"Thanks," Jordan said.

"Samira's mom was in my office for a check-up today."

Jordan searched her mom's face in the mirror's reflection. She worried that her mother had heard about the shove at practice.

"She told me that you've quit the basketball team," her mom said.

Jordan wrapped the cord around the curling iron and put it back in the drawer.

"I thought you loved basketball," her mom said.

"I do."

Her mom shook her head. "Why would you quit something you love?"

Jordan's eyes watered. Now was not the time to cry into her mascara.

"You're going to let someone else decide who you are?"

"What choice do I have?" Jordan said.

"You always have a choice." Her mom stepped into the bathroom and straightened Jordan's hairclip. "There's always *something* you can do."

"That's not what you said."

Her mom jerked her head back. "Me? What did I say?"

"You said that that's the way the world works."

"Oh, that." Her mom's face softened. "Sometimes I get a little carried away. It's not quite as bad as I said. I mean, just look at your dad. He believes girls should play sports. If he didn't, he wouldn't have spent all those hours in the yard with you."

"That's just because I'm his daughter," Jordan said.

"I don't think so," said her mom. "Besides, if nobody ever tries to change how the world works, then the world will never change."

"I'm not feeling up to changing the world, Mom."

"I haven't told your dad yet about your quitting basketball," said her mom. "But you know he'll feel very sad for you."

Then the doorbell rang and Jordan could hear the murmur of Amin's voice talking to her dad. It was time for her first date.

★★★

It was dark on the drive out to the University of British Columbia. Jordan and Amin sat in the back while Amin's father drove. Jordan didn't know what to talk about as they drove up the highway. To her relief, Amin's father, Mr. Haddad, did most of the talking.

"Should be a good game tonight," he said. "Against Calgary. Amin's sister, Noora, put up fifteen points last time they played Calgary."

Jordan watched the lights of the greenhouses pass by in the darkness. "What position is Noora?" she asked.

"Shooting guard," Amin said. "One of the best in the league."

"Do you plan to play in university?" Mr. Haddad glanced at Jordan through the rearview mirror.

Jordan felt a swell of regret. There was nothing in the world more exciting to Jordan than the thought of playing at that level. But that couldn't happen if she didn't play ball in high school.

"Yeah, maybe," she said. She wished she could go back to being the person who dribbled her basketball all the way to school every morning, not caring one bit what anyone thought.

The university was like a miniature city. Jordan loved the old stone of the buildings and how the ivy vines covered whole walls. As they walked to the game, crowds of students walked in the same direction, cheering and blowing horns. They were all dressed in their university colours, blue and gold.

When they got to the gym, Mr. Haddad said, "Meet me here after the game." Then he went off to find his own seat.

Suddenly Amin and Jordan were alone for the first time that night.

"Come on," Amin said. "There's something I want to get for you."

They wove through the crowd in the lobby area until they reached a small booth. Amin bought Jordan a game program with his own money. On the front of the program was a young woman leaping for a shot. Her face wore a grimace of intensity.

"That," Amin tapped the program cover, "is my sister."

"Really?" Jordan was amazed.

"We'll get Noora to sign it for you after the game," he said.

The stands were filled with fans. Amin and Jordan found good seats near the middle of the court. During the warmup, Jordan's gaze was fixed on the players. Their skills — dribbling, shooting, passing — were top-notch. It gave Jordan a picture of what she could become someday if she kept playing.

As the players gathered at their benches before the starting tipoff, the crowd chanted for their home team.

"THUN-DER-BIRDS! THUN-DER-BIRDS!"

Amin pumped his fist in the air and joined the chant. Jordan felt too shy to do the same. But Amin grinned at her and chanted even louder, as if he'd rather have fun than care about looking silly in front of her. Jordan clapped her hands along with the chant like some of the other fans.

From the first jump ball, Jordan was right in the game. She thrilled by the echo of squeaking shoes and the thud of the basketball. She watched closely as Number 5, the point guard for the UBC Thunderbirds, brought the ball up the court. The defender on the Calgary Dinos mirrored Number 5's movements in a perfect defensive stance. Her feet were quick, and her watchful eyes determined.

Number 5 stood dribbling in one spot at the top of the three-point line. She called out the play loudly. Then she shouted, "Move it, move it, that's it, that's it!"

Number 5 wasn't the only one shouting things. Many of the players communicated with each other. Calling for the ball, telling each other what to do as they quickly moved into their positions. They were constantly cutting this way and that, never stopping their motion, always jostling against their defenders. And when the ball went up for a shot, the women went hard for the rebound.

Jordan clenched her fists tightly with excitement. The women were so bold and confident and strong. They even wore proper uniforms, the type Jordan had wanted for her team. Jordan wanted to be just like these players. Sure, she'd watched women's basketball on TV. But to see it right in front of her eyes dazzled her.

Jordan watched as Noora sank a three-pointer that was so perfect the net barely moved. Amin and Jordan gave each other a high five. She wondered why

Number 5 was the team captain and not Noora. But before she could ask, Amin shouted into her ear over the noise of the crowd.

"Just you wait. She's only getting started!"

Sure enough, Noora drained three-pointer after three-pointer. By the final buzzer, the Thunderbirds had beat the Calgary Dinos 72–68.

17 ROLE MODELS

Jordan noticed the women on the team hugging each other and giving high fives. And she felt like she'd lost something. There was nothing like being a part of a team. She thought of how excited her own team had been for her when she became the top scorer in the league. She thought of how happy she felt when Mayleen scored all those points in the game against the Newton Rockets. She laughed to herself when she thought how her team shared the misery of doing lines at the start of every practice.

Jordan wondered if she'd made a mistake. She wasn't being herself if she didn't play basketball. But how could she go back and change her mind now? Besides, there was Wyatt Nowack and everyone else's opinions of her. She couldn't handle it anymore. Things were easier if she didn't play basketball.

Next thing Jordan knew, Amin was taking her down the aisle to the court. The floor was so shiny that Jordan wanted to reach down and feel it with her fingers. They went to the Thunderbirds bench. Up close, Jordan noticed that all the players were drenched in sweat.

"Noora," said Amin, "this is my friend, Jordan."

Noora shook Jordan's hand. Her palm was sweaty, but Jordan didn't care.

"I hear you play basketball, too," Noora said. She motioned at her brother with her water bottle. "Amin says you're an amazing dribbler with a wicked three-point shot."

Amin said, "Too bad she's not playing ball anymore."

"Seriously?" Noora pulled the towel off the back of her neck. "How come? I thought you were the team captain."

Jordan didn't know what to say.

"It's sad to me, how many girls quit sports around your age," Noora said. "Let me guess. You're too busy with a billion other things. Swimming lessons, homework, maybe a part-time job?"

"No, not really," Jordan said.

"Then it must be boys," Noora said.

Jordan looked at Amin, whose face turned pink.

"She didn't quit because of me," Amin said. Then he turned to Jordan. "You didn't, did you?"

Jordan laughed and shook her head.

Noora smiled. "No, not boys like you, Amin. What I mean is the idea of what you need to be for boys to like you. Don't sweat, don't grunt, don't get dirty, don't try hard. And heaven forbid, don't show even a teensy shred of muscle."

"And don't beat a boy in basketball," Jordan added.

"Definitely not that!" Noora laughed.

"You have no idea how many times I was called 'butch' for being so into sports," she continued. "I mean, really? I suddenly look like a man because I love to throw an orange orb into a ring?"

Jordan chuckled. Noora had a point.

"I almost quit many times at your age because of it," Noora said.

"You did?" Amin said. "I can't believe you've *ever* thought of quitting."

"Too many days of crying my eyes out." Noora put her hand on Jordan's shoulder. "Take it from me, a ball player just like you. You don't need to choose between feeling like a girl — whatever *that* means — and playing sports. You understand what I'm saying?"

Jordan nodded.

"Things won't ever get perfect," Noora went on. "There'll always be some jerk who will bully you —"

"Wyatt Nowack."

"Wyatt bullies you?" Amin asked.

"You've heard the way he calls me a jock," Jordan said.

"I never knew that bothered you," Amin said. "I would've said something."

"There'll always be Wyatt Nowacks in the world," Noora said. "Other people who try to tell you who you are. But things do get better, I promise."

"Thanks," Jordan said. "But that doesn't really help much now."

"I remember when I was your age. This boy, Freddie, teased me about being a jock," Noora said. "I asked him why he was teasing me about being good at sports. He said it was because girls could never be as good as boys. In front of his friends I asked him if he was worried that I might be as good as he was and if that's why he was teasing me. He stopped. See, people only cut you down because they are worried, because you are good."

"Not sure I could say that," Jordan said.

Noora shrugged. "Then just *show* them how good you are. That's all you can do."

Amin pointed to the program in Jordan's hand. "Noora, will you autograph it?"

Noora grabbed a pen from her coach's clipboard and signed her picture on the program cover. It read:

Don't ever quit, Jordan. Noora Haddad #7

"Don't let others define who you are," Noora said. "Only you get to do that."

Jordan nodded.

"Guess we better find Dad," Amin said. He gave his sister a tight hug. "Great game."

As Amin and Jordan started to walk away, Jordan

turned back to Noora. "How come you're not the captain, Noora?" she asked. "You're the best player out there."

"You don't always pick the best player to be captain," Noora said. "You pick the player who is the best leader." She gestured at Number 5, the point guard who'd led all the plays. "For us, that's Sarah Sanderson. Takes a special person to be the leader."

As they walked through the parking lot, Jordan asked Amin, "Do you think your sister will turn pro? I bet she'll get a contract offer. How could any team pass her up?"

"I agree," Amin said. "Maybe she'll even get some sponsorship offers."

"Yeah, like for deodorant," Jordan said, and they both burst out laughing.

They piled into the backseat of the car. Amin's dad muttered as he wove through the stop-and-go traffic out of the parking lot.

"I loved that jump shot Noora did at the end of the second!" Jordan said. She lifted her arms in an imitation. Then let her hands fall beside her, lost for a moment in the memory.

Amin put his hand on top of hers.

Jordan stiffened slightly. Amin's hand was warm and smooth. She looked sideways toward Amin but he was looking straight ahead.

"I wish I could play as well as my sister," Amin

said. "She is such a good athlete. She taught me everything I know about basketball."

"Didn't it bother you to be taught by your sister?" asked Jordan.

"Of course not. My sister's an amazing player."

"So, if she showed you how to dribble behind your back, you wouldn't care?"

Amin screwed up his face. "Why would I care?"

Jordan turned her hand so her palm was facing up. She closed it around Amin's.

She thought about how Noora had faced the same kind of bullying she had. Even though it was painful to recall, Jordan sorted through all the things that had been said about her at school. That she was a jock. That she wasn't really a girl. That she was gay. That she was too manly. She imagined how Noora might have handled all those situations. Would it have been better if Jordan had faced the taunts and defended herself? Or was it better to walk away and not encourage them?

"Your sister has guts," Jordan said. She thought about how brave Noora acted in her story about Freddie.

"Yeah, but she's always been like that. That's just her," Amin said. "She's a real leader, even if she's not the captain."

During her games, Jordan would keep an eye out for players who were getting tired or frustrated. She'd encourage them, saying things like, "Don't give up, you can do it," and "I know you're tired, but let's keep fighting." That was what being a leader was about. It took a special person to be a leader, that's what Noora had said. Good leaders helped people to keep going.

But who keeps the leaders going? Jordan wondered.

She knew the answer. It wasn't the women on the deodorant commercials. It was heroes like Diana Taurasi. It was role models like Noora Haddad. It was her teammates.

As they finally pulled into Jordan's driveway, she thanked Mr. Haddad for the ride and said, "See you at the big game tomorrow, Mr. Haddad."

Amin's face lit up. "You're going to come to watch?"

Smiling, Jordan shook her head.

"I'm going to come to play."

18 Old FRIENDS

Jordan woke up. Instantly she was filled with both dread and excitement. Today was the big day. The pep rally. The rematch against the Mavericks. But before all that, she had to find the courage to talk to Coach Banford. And then she'd have to face the team. She didn't know what to tell them.

Classes seemed to drag on forever. Jordan wished it all was behind her and that she was playing basketball right then. She played the scene of addressing the team over and over in her head. And the conversation with Coach Banford. She couldn't imagine them saying no to her. But she couldn't be sure. And even if she was back on the team, would they still want her to be captain?

Jordan thought it would never come, but finally the lunch bell rang. Before she lost her nerve, she headed straight for Coach Banford's classroom. The door was open and she could see her coach sitting at the desk, probably marking papers. Jordan knocked and he looked up.

"Can I talk to you?" she asked.

He motioned to the chair closest to the desk.

Jordan's heart felt like it was in her throat. That morning, as she dribbled her basketball all the way to school, she'd rehearsed a hundred times what she'd say to him. Sitting in front of him now, she struggled to gather her thoughts. Finally, she blurted out the truth.

"I shouldn't have quit the team."

He put down the pen and folded his hands. "What changed?"

"I just changed my mind," Jordan said.

"Look, Jordan, I know about Wyatt."

Jordan gazed at the desk.

"He's just a poor sport," Coach Banford said. "I could talk to him if you want."

"No, thanks. There'll always be boys like him."

"All right. Well, I'm glad to have you back on the team." Coach looked pleased.

"I was also wondering if I'm still —"

"The team didn't want to pick another captain," Coach Banford said. "They were hoping you'd change your mind."

"There's one other thing," Jordan said. "The uniforms."

"What about them?"

"I'm not comfortable in them." Jordan shifted in her chair.

"Your team picked them," Coach Banford said.

"They picked them for boys. Not for basketball."

Coach Banford chuckled.

Jordan narrowed her eyes. She didn't see what was so funny about it.

"It's not just the girls," Coach Banford said. "Trust me, the boys also worry about looking good on the court."

"The boys want to look like good players. They worry about *basketball* on the court. Because they're supposed to."

"Aren't the girls supposed to?" Coach Banford asked.

"No, we're not supposed to. We don't get to."

Coach Banford looked puzzled.

"Mostly because of TV," Jordan said.

Coach Banford scrunched his eyebrows even lower. "The girls picked those uniforms because of TV?"

"And movies. Magazines. Stuff on the Internet." Jordan remembered Noora's words. "Don't sweat, don't grunt, don't get dirty, don't try hard. And heaven forbid, don't show even a teensy shred of muscle."

Coach Banford's face softened. "Is this why you quit? The uniforms?"

Jordan shook her head. "I'd play basketball in orange garbage bags if I had to."

"I'm not sure there's anything I can do about it now," Coach Banford said. "You'll have to wait until you're on the senior team over in the other building.

They've got proper basketball uniforms."

"I know nothing can be done about it now," Jordan said. She didn't know how to explain it to Coach Banford. That she needed to prove to herself that she had the guts to say something. Like Noora would. "It's just that I want to say —" Jordan was unsure of her words. "It's just that —" She stood up. "I should get to feel dressed to play."

***

Jordan went straight from Coach Banford's classroom to the gym. At one end, the badminton club was playing. At the other was a lone player shooting baskets. It was Samira. They hadn't talked since Jordan had shoved Samira at the practice. Jordan was surprised to see her practising at lunch.

Without saying a word, Jordan stood under the hoop and waited. Samira took a shot and scored. Jordan passed the ball back to her. Samira shot again and scored a second time. She seemed to be back to her old way of moving, and she was back to trying hard. When Jordan passed the ball, Samira dribbled toward the net and passed it to Jordan for a shot.

For fifteen minutes, they played like that in silence, passing and shooting. It was just like all those summer days they had spent together, playing through the afternoon and evening in Jordan's driveway.

"Heard you went on a date with Amin," Samira said.

"To a basketball game at UBC. His sister was playing." Jordan took a shot from the free-throw line.

"Wyatt and I went on a date, too," Samira said.

Jordan detected something off about Samira's voice. "How did it go?"

"Oh, great," Samira said. "If you're into listening to a jerk talk about himself for three hours straight. He didn't even stop to watch the movie. Just kept on talking about how great he was at basketball. And motocross racing. And blah, blah, blah. He didn't ask me one single thing about myself. It was the most boring date I've ever been on."

"It's the only date you've ever been on," Jordan said, smiling.

Samira laughed. "That doesn't make it any less true."

"Well, I'm sorry it went so badly," Jordan said. She realized she meant it. "Also —" Jordan felt a swell of embarrassment. "I'm very sorry I pushed you like that."

Samira waved her hand at Jordan as if to say it was no big deal. "I'm the one who should be sorry. Just standing there saying nothing while he insulted you like that."

Jordan shrugged. "It's okay."

"No, it's not," Samira insisted. "And now you're not on the team anymore."

"I'm back on the team," said Jordan.

"For real?" Samira grinned.

"Just talked to Coach Banford."

"Tonight's game is going to be incredible," Samira said.

"It's going to be so loud in here," Jordan agreed.

"Plus, the big pep rally this afternoon," Samira added.

"Better than Math class," Jordan said.

Samira's eyes lit up. "Wait. Does the rest of the team know yet?"

"Not yet."

Samira threw the basketball into the ball bin. "We should go tell them right now. Most of them are in the cafeteria."

19 PEP RALLY

As the girls changed into their uniforms, they could hear the whole school in the gym. Principal Young was leading a cheer.

"Hey-o! Hey-o-o!"

They heard the crowd of students repeating Principal Young's call at the top of their lungs. At the same time, they stomped their feet in rhythm on the bleachers. The sound thundered through the change room walls.

"This is so exciting!" Hazel said.

"I'm nervous," Samira admitted.

"Me too," Petra said.

Jordan didn't bother to stretch out her uniform this time. Instead, she imagined she was wearing the kind of uniform she wanted. It was all she could do for now.

When the girls were ready, they went out into the hall so that Coach Banford could explain how the pep rally would go. "You'll wait here in a line," he told them. "Principal Young will introduce each player to the school on the microphone. When you hear your name, you'll run across the court and stand with the rest of your team. This is your moment, girls. Enjoy it."

Jordan stood along the wall between Samira and Hazel. She was thrilled to be taking part in this day. She would have shriveled up inside if she had to watch her team from the stands.

At the end of the hall was the entrance to the gym. From where she stood, Jordan could see that the gym lights were turned off. Red and blue and yellow lights flashed and turned in long beams. It was just like when the pro teams were introduced to the crowd before a game. Jordan had heard there was even going to be a fog machine.

Coach Li and the boys' team emerged from the other change room farther down the hall. They lined up against the wall opposite the girls.

Jordan smiled at Amin, who looked nervous. She gave him a thumbs up.

Then she spotted Wyatt. He was busy straightening his shorts and tucking in his jersey. She thought of how he'd shouted "Jordan the Jock" from the bleachers the last time they played the Mavericks. How he'd managed to get some of his teammates to chant it with him. She also thought of how some of the other kids in her school had started to call her Jordan the Jock.

Jordan suddenly felt sick to her stomach. What was

going to happen when Principal Young introduced her? She imagined the cheers turning into a chant of "Jordan the Jock" from the entire school.

They were about to start the introductions. There was no going back now, was there?

The girls' team was introduced first. Principal Young really hammed it up, revving up his voice like he was announcing a monster-truck rally.

"Orcas forward, number 13 . . . Petra Stone!!!!"

All the players in the hall — girls and boys — clapped for Petra and encouraged her to run out.

"Whooo, Petra! Way to go!"

Mayleen went next. Then Tara.

As the line shuffled forward, Jordan's palms sweated. She truly worried she might throw up. She braced herself for embarrassment. The only thing she could do was try her best to ignore any chants and keep a straight face.

The only girls left were Samira, Hazel and Jordan.

Samira was introduced next, then Hazel.

"Just Jordan the Jock, and then it's our turn, boys," Wyatt said.

"Knock it off, Wyatt." Amin moved out of his place in line to face Wyatt.

"Okay, relax," Wyatt said. "I'm just joking around."

"Well, it's not funny," Amin said.

Wyatt threw up his hands as if to say he surrendered.

Principal Young called out on the microphone.

"And finally, the player you've all been waiting for. Point guard and captain of the Orcas. One of the top scorers in the entire league . . . Number 11, Jordan Connor!!"

The roar of the crowd was ten times louder than for any of the other introductions. Jordan tingled from her head to her feet. She took a deep breath and ran into the gym. She ran through the smoke from the fog machine and through the whirling red, blue and yellow lights.

It was dizzying. The feeling was unlike anything she'd ever felt before. Through the darkness, she could feel the energy of the crowd, though she could only catch glimpses of the students as the lights panned across the bleachers.

That was when she saw it. Some of her classmates — she couldn't see who — had made a big poster for the famous player from the Chicago Bulls, Michael Jordan. But when she looked closely, she saw it wasn't about Michael Jordan at all.

We love ~~Michael~~ Jordan!!!

Jordan smiled. Someone had taken the time to make a poster just for her. She waved at the crowd as she stood next to her teammates. As excited as she was, though, Jordan still braced herself for the sound of "Jordan the Jock."

"That is unbelievable!" Samira shouted to Jordan.

"Totally!" Jordan said.

Before the boys were introduced, Ms. Murray sprinted into the gym. Everybody burst into laughter. She was wearing a huge orca costume. When she moved her feet, the orca's fluke wiggled back and forth. She waved her fins at the crowd.

"OR-CAS! OR-CAS! OR-CAS!" the crowd chanted.

The girls' team joined the cheer. As Jordan watched Ms. Murray, she thought again about the *GSA* pamphlet. No longer would Jordan worry about why Ms. Murray gave it to her. For one thing, Ms. Murray wasn't the type to make assumptions about people. And she wasn't the type to be dishonest. If she said it was about serving the school, then that was what it was about. But besides that, Jordan realized that Noora was right.

Nobody gets to define who I am. Except me, she thought.

When the boys were introduced, Jordan whooped and hollered as loud as she could when Amin's name was announced. Like Jordan, as captain of the team, Wyatt was introduced last. But Principal Young didn't give Wyatt as good an introduction as he had for Jordan.

"And finally, shooting guard and captain of the boys' team . . . Number 12, Wyatt Nowack!!"

Samira leaned over and said, "Booo," in Jordan's ear.

Jordan nodded at her best friend and rolled her eyes.

Then both of them did their part and applauded Wyatt's entrance.

★★★

"That was the best day of my life," Samira said when the pep rally was over.

Jordan still felt the waves of relief that had washed over her. Not one person had called out "Jordan the Jock."

"I'm so glad I didn't quit basketball," said Samira.

"Me too," said Jordan.

"Did you see that sign with your name on it?" Samira asked. "I wonder who it was. I can't even imagine someone going to the trouble of making a sign for me. I bet they bring your sign to the game."

"I hope so," Jordan said. She liked the thought of her dad seeing the sign. "Maybe it'll help us win tonight. Every little thing helps."

20 The Big REMATCH

Jordan laced up her basketball shoes slowly. She filled her mind with visions of the ball going through the net. She pictured herself powering down the court. She saw herself dribbling the ball as though it was tied to her hand with an invisible string. She imagined leaping high in the air to snatch a rebound. All the best players, she'd once read, visualized the game before stepping onto the court.

In the gym, the crowd was as loud as it had been that afternoon at the pep rally. It was even more packed now, with parents and other relatives, plus some Mavericks fans, filling the place. In fact, it was so packed that people had to stand beside the bleachers to watch.

The girls played first. It still bugged Jordan, that the girls' game was a kind of warmup act for the supposedly more important boys' game. But she was too excited to worry too much about it tonight.

During the warmup, Jordan noticed Mavericks Number 10 glancing at her several times. Shawna Yee.

Jordan remembered her name from the league website. Shawna was still the top scorer, ahead of Jordan by about eight points. When Jordan dribbled around the outside perimeter, Shawna nodded her head at Jordan. Jordan nodded back. Two of the top players acknowledging one another.

Coach Banford gave a short pregame talk. He sounded as pumped as Jordan felt. "This is going to be an intense game, girls. I'm not going to say much to you right now. Except enjoy yourselves out there. Play hard. Have fun."

The girls put their fists into the centre of the huddle. "Go, Orcas!"

Stepping onto the court, Jordan scanned the bleachers. She couldn't find Amin. He wasn't sitting with his team. But she spotted her dad in the lower section. Right above him was a sign, the same one from the pep rally. Two classmates from her Art class were waving it wildly in the air.

Hazel lost the opening tipoff and the Orcas scrambled back onto defence. Samira was checking Shawna Yee. Unlike her recent games, Samira was a workhorse tonight. She stayed low to the ball, shuffling her feet rapidly. Shawna couldn't get past Samira. With no one open, Shawna forced an outside shot that rebounded hard off the backboard. Mayleen grabbed the ball and targeted Jordan for an outlet pass.

Jordan spotted Samira racing up the court alone.

She threw a long baseball pass. It landed perfectly in front of Samira, who took a step and drove up to the basket. And scored. The crowd leaped to their feet and cheered.

The next time down the court, Jordan pretended to eye a player down low. Instead, she pulled up a three-pointer and drained it.

"Three!!!!!!" the crowd shouted.

Samira continued to play Shawna Yee tightly. At one point in the second quarter, Samira managed to steal the ball from Shawna. "Our new play!" Samira shouted to Jordan as they sprinted up the court. Samira drove the ball down low to pull the defence away from Jordan. Jordan sprinted around Samira, using her as a pick to lose her own check. She circled back out high and Samira sent a bullet of a pass to the outside perimeter. Jordan pulled up another three-pointer.

Swish!

Cries of disbelief erupted from the crowd. Jordan had sunk four out of five three-point attempts. She was on fire. Their whole team was on fire. By half-time, Orcas were up 28–20.

"Keep it up, Samira," Jordan said. "You're completely shutting down Number 10. She's hardly scored."

Before heading back onto the court, Jordan scanned the bleachers once more. From the bottom corner, right next to the sideline, Amin waved to get her attention. Sitting on one side of Amin was his dad. Once Amin saw that he had her attention, he pointed excitedly to the person sitting on his other side.

It was his sister, Noora.

Jordan's mouth fell open. Her mind raced back to everything she could remember about the first half. She wanted to figure out exactly what Noora Haddad had seen. Four three-pointers, for starters! Two great breakaways with Samira. Tons of great passes. But most of all, she hoped that Noora had seen Jordan being the best leader on the court she could be.

With Noora in the crowd, Jordan started playing her heart out even more than in the first half. Coming down the court, she called out the play louder than usual. The Orcas whipped the ball around the perimeter with lightning speed, then reversed it. Jordan went to pull up another three-pointer. Her check moved on her quickly, so Jordan faked the shot and dribbled around her. From the top of the paint, she spotted Hazel down low and passed off the ball.

After Hazel scored, she pointed at Jordan to thank her for the pass. Jordan clapped hard as she jogged backward to get set up on defence. "Keep it going, Orcas! No quitting now!"

As the clock wound down at the end of the game, the crowd counted down. "Ten, nine, eight, seven, six, five, four, three, two, one!"

The buzzer went. The crowd cheered. The Orcas

congratulated each other on their 62–48 win.

Jordan waved at her dad and signaled that she'd be over to sit with him in a few minutes. First, she wanted to take Samira to the bleachers to meet Noora. Jordan and Samira sat with Noora and watched the boys warm up.

"You two are a pair of dynamos," Noora said. "You make a great team. Some pretty sweet plays you've worked out."

"Thanks," said Jordan. "We practice a lot together."

"Glad to see you didn't quit, Jordan," said Noora. "You have a big future in basketball."

Jordan beamed.

Wyatt ran to the sidelines to grab a rolling ball. "Nice game, Jock."

"Shut it, Wyatt," Samira said.

Wyatt jerked his head back. "I said, *nice* game."

Noora stood up, staring hard at Wyatt. He stared back, looking a little unsure of himself. She walked up to him, took the ball from his hands and launched a long shot all the way from the sidelines. It went right through the hoop. Some of the boys on the court noticed and turned, their mouths gaping. Amin smiled and said something to one of his teammates.

Wyatt stood there, looking dumbfounded.

"Better get your ball and get warmed up, kid," Noora said.

Samira nudged Jordan in the ribs. Both of them chuckled.

Noora turned to Jordan. "See? Sometimes all you can do is to *show* them how good you are. And keep showing them."

Watching the boys' game with Samira and Noora, Jordan felt lighter than she had in weeks. As long as there were boys like Wyatt in the school, she knew that things would not change overnight. It meant being true to herself, it meant not letting others crush her passion. But she could bear it. Not to mention how much more bearable it would be with the support of other girls and women like Samira and Noora — and boys like Amin.

★★★

Jordan was about to leave the school, but she had something she wanted to do first. Alone in the hall, she opened her locker door. She took tape out of her duffel bag and carefully put her magazine cut-outs of Diana Taurasi back up. Except this time, she left an empty space in the middle. She carefully taped up a special picture she'd cut out at home. It was the Thunderbirds program cover with the photo of Noora. Jordan read Noora's message to her.

Don't ever quit, Jordan. Noora Haddad #7

Jordan took out her basketball and shut her locker door.

ACKNOWLEDGEMENTS

Special thanks to the Kyuquot Kakawins basketball team, the most amazing group of girls I've ever coached.

To Kat Mototsune and all the staff at Lorimer.

To Lorna Schultz Nicholson for her personal support and for her own sports books, which I have loved over the years.

Most importantly, to every girl who has ever felt as though she is not a "real" girl just because she sweats, builds muscles and loves her sport more than anything. Never let others define who and what you are. And never quit.

Check out these exciting, action-packed books from Lorimer's Sports Stories series:

Tough Call

By Kelsey Blair

In need of money to pay her basketball fees, fourteen-year old Malia King registers for a refereeing course at her middle school. Refereeing gives her a whole new perspective on the game, and helps to improve her own play. But things get complicated when Malia is assigned to referee her younger sister Flo's games, especially when she makes a call that leads to a big loss for her school. As people around Malia start pressuring her to favour the team from her own school she has to choose between calling a fair game or becoming a social outcast.

Bad Shot

By Sylvia Taekema

Twelve-year-old Cody loves basketball. When a new well-off kid Nick arrives at school and starts giving Cody pointers, Cody lands a spot on the team. Despite Nick's help, Cody still feels anxious all the time. Cody's performance gets worse until his one big shot at a basket goes into his own team's net! Cody soon realizes that Nick's help isn't what he needs to succeed. To play better, he knows he has to become more self-reliant and work on his basketball skills on his own terms.

Set against the realistic backdrop of a struggling small town, Bad Shot touches on the emotional realities of performance anxiety, socioeconomic status, and bullying.

Hoop Magic

By Eric Howling

Orlando O'Malley has had to overcome a lot to play basketball. He's the worst shooter on the Evergreen Eagles middle school team. He can barely dribble around a cone in practice. And he's certainly the shortest. But Orlando has two special talents: a winning personality and the ability to call play-by-play almost everything that is happening around him.

Orlando really wants to be a star player, but despite his best efforts he can't quite seem to make the right play at the right time. His biggest contributions to the team are his ability to get them energized and to call the shots. But accepting these as his special talents means he has to give up his dream of playing basketball.

Making the Team

By Kelsey Blair

When Hannah doesn't make the Grade 8 girls basketball team and her best friend June does, Hannah misses playing basketball and being part of a team. Worse, she and June don't spend as much time together and start growing apart. How can Hannah ensure that she makes the team next year while all the other players are playing more and getting better this year? As she develops her basketball skills and confidence, she realizes she stands a good shot at making the high school team. But can she ever get her friendship with June back?

M
MARQUIS
Québec, Canada